TAL
His Marvellous Adventures
with
Noom-Zor-Noom

A

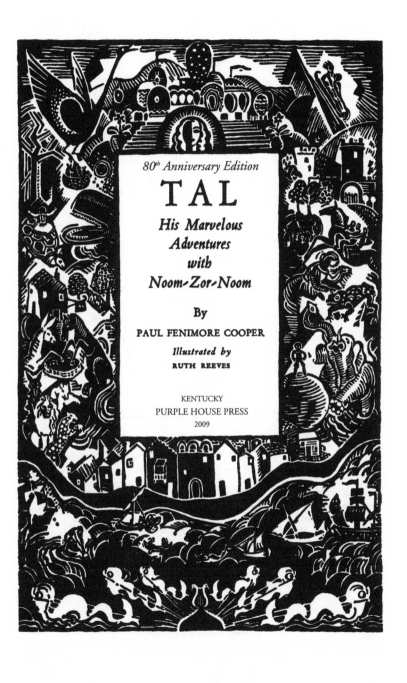

80th *Anniversary Edition*

TAL

*His Marvelous
Adventures
with
Noom-Zor-Noom*

By

PAUL FENIMORE COOPER

Illustrated by
RUTH REEVES

KENTUCKY
PURPLE HOUSE PRESS
2009

Published by
Purple House Press
PO Box 787, Cynthiana, Kentucky 41031
www.PurpleHousePress.com

Publisher's Cataloging-in-Publication Data

Cooper, Paul Fenimore.
TAL. His Marvelous Adventures with Noom-Zor-Noom;
illustrated by Ruth Reeves.
p. cm.
Summary: The story of Tal, a young orphan, and the adventures that befall
him on the amazing journey to the land of Troom. His companions are the
wise old man Noom-Zor-Noom and the talking donkey Millitinkle.
ISBN 978-1-930900-41-7 (paperback : alk. paper)
[1. Fantasy.   2. Adventure.   3. Folk Tales.]
I. Reeves, Ruth, ill. II. Title.
PZ8.C792 Tal3 2009   [Fic]–dc22   2009905052

Printed in the United States of America
1 2 3 4 5 6 7 8 9 10
First Paperback Edition

To

KATHERINE
and
SUSAN

INTRODUCTION

TAL, His Marvelous Adventures with Noom-Zor-Noom, has had a considerable following since its publication in 1929 and its reissue in 1957. Though out of print most of the years since then, it is something of a classic that has had a loyal and steadfast readership. Generations of young people grew up and read this magical book to their children and grandchildren, passing down through the decades their devotion to white-bearded Noom-Zor-Noom with his black crystal block covered with gold-lettered tales, the boy Tal who will know the best story when he hears it, and the clever donkey Millitinkle with bells in her pink ears who carries the heavy crystal block on their journey.

Paul Fenimore Cooper, a consummate story teller, is himself the descendant of several generations of men and women who wrote. His great-great-grandfather, William Cooper, who founded Cooperstown, New York, the village where Paul Cooper spent most of his life, wrote *A Guide in the Wilderness,* published in 1810, an account of the settling of this rural community which is itself something of a classic in the pioneering literature of this country. Paul's great-grandfather, James Fenimore Cooper, who grew up in this village on the shore of Otsego Lake, the Glimmerglass of *The Deerslayer,* was the novelist of the American wilderness whose works helped define this country's view of nature for many generations. His great aunt, Susan Fenimore Cooper, was the author of *Rural Hours,* a journal published in

1850, covering a year in the still young settlement of Cooperstown, with a particular interest in how nature changes through the seasons; Thoreau had a copy of it in his cabin at Walden Pond. Paul's own father, another James Fenimore Cooper, in his history, *The Legends and Traditions of a Northern County,* published in 1921, was also a storyteller about the people and places in this region.

Since his home town had been so thoroughly worked over by his forebears, Paul went further afield. After graduating from Yale in 1921 and spending some time at Trinity College in Cambridge, he went on a walking trip in Albania, where he became entranced with that country's rich folk tales. Many of these he published in *Tricks of Women* in 1928. The fantasy of Tal and Noom-Zor-Noom may owe something to his time in Albania.

TAL, first published in 1929, appeared at the same time A.A. Milne was writing the Pooh books, Hugh Lofting was turning out the Dr. Doolittle books, and Walter R. Brooks was writing about Freddy the Pig. A couple of years later, Laurent de Brunhoff began writing about Babar. All these books differed from *TAL* in that they were about talking animals who were surrogates for people; they were fantasies with one foot in the real world. Though Millitinkle might have been happy in the Big Woods with Eeyore, *TAL* was about a fairy tale world. Another contemporary, L. Frank Baum, in his Oz books, was writing about a fairy tale world, too, but it was a world with a strong Kansas flavor. *TAL* was much closer to the world of Grimm and Hans Christian Anderson – and to the Albanian tradition Paul Cooper was familiar with, which had something about it of the Arabian Nights.

But this type of book was to have tougher sledding, particularly after World War II, when child psychologists considered children too delicate for fairy tales which they believed undermined a child's grip on reality. Rather, the new post-war fashion in children's books was that they be user-friendly, pragmatic, practical and deal with real life situations. Pooh and Babar made the grade; so did Dorothy and her mid-western Oz, but Little Red Riding Hood – and Tal – had it tougher.

I can remember Paul Cooper, who was my uncle, complaining about the lack of imagination which pervaded children's literature in the 'forties, 'fifties, and 'sixties. With a few exceptions (such as the works of J.R.R. Tolkien, whose *Lord of the Rings* was written for grownups), this fairy tale wasteland lasted past Paul's death in 1970; it didn't begin to turn around until psychologists and psychiatrists such as Bruno Bettelheim in *The Uses of Enchantment: The Meaning and Importance of Fairy Tales* (1976) rediscovered the fact that fairy tales resonated with the rich fantasy life of children, and that children loved them. The generations of youngsters and grownups who have kept *TAL* alive throughout the last seventy years are a testament to this fact. *TAL* in recent years has emerged on the Internet, on the websites of virtual bookstores, as one of the most sought-after out-of-print children's books. Now, at the insistence of its readers, *TAL* is reborn.

Katherine and Susan, to whom the book is dedicated, are Paul Cooper's nieces (and my older sisters). They were seven and nine when *TAL* was written. They remember their uncle reading the book to them, as if he were Noom-Zor-Noom, and they are looking forward to reading the new edition of their book to their own grandchildren.

But it is time to stop talking about *TAL*. It casts its own spell, and who can account for that?

Henry S.F. Cooper, Jr.
Cooperstown, N.Y.

CONTENTS

CONTENTS

TAL

His Marvellous Adventures
with
Noom-Zor-Noom

CHAPTER I

TAL, THE BOY WITH THE GOLDEN HAIR, AND HOW HE MET NOOM-ZOR-NOOM AND THE DONKEY CALLED MILLITINKLE

FAR AWAY on the other side of the sea there once was a village called Martoona. It was built on a steep hillside at the foot of some high mountains. Below the village was a wide, sandy beach—then the sea. All the houses in the village were white with red tile roofs, and the streets were steep and narrow and were paved with big cobblestones. There was a marketplace where the people bought and sold; there was a blacksmith's shop, a cobbler's shop, and a tinker's shop. But most of the men spent their time fishing, for the sea was full of the most wonderful fish. And ships from all over the world came to Martoona to load with fish, for which the captains paid big prices. So the people in the village made a good living and were happy.

In Martoona there was a poor boy named Tal. At least, that was the name the people in the village gave him. He really did not have any name of his own, because he had no father or mother and no one knew where he came from. Of course there were many stories of how he had come to Martoona. Some said he had been left by the captain of a boat. Some said that a bird had brought him. And others said that he had been washed up on the beach in a cradle. But all these were just stories—that's all. The truth is that one evening Tal was *not* there, and the next morning he *was*. More than that no one really knew.

Tal was a little boy then, hardly more than a year old. And the people of Martoona, being kind people, took good care of him. The butcher, I think, was the first to take him in. But the butcher was poor and he had children of his own. So he kept Tal for only a short time. Then the cobbler took care of him for a while, then the blacksmith, then the tinker, then the miller, and then a lot of other people. In this way Tal spent his early childhood, now with one family, now with another. And every one who took care of Tal liked him, he was so good, so kind, and so well behaved. He was never a nuisance to any one. When he got a little older, he used to work for the people who took care of him. He ran their errands, he did this, he did that, he did everything he could to repay them for their kindness. Of course they liked him all the more for this. And no one could be found who had a bad word to say about Tal, the village boy of Martoona.

Time passed; Tal grew up. When he was nine years old, all the people thought they had never seen so beautiful a boy. He had big blue eyes, bright red cheeks, and his hair was golden yellow. His friends talked about him so much and so often, that strangers who came to

Martoona were not long in finding out all about Tal. When these strangers went back to their homes, they told their friends what they had heard of the boy. Thus Tal became known to many, many people whom he had never seen or met. And all over the world, in every house, could be found some one who knew of Tal, the boy with the golden hair.

Tal might well have gone on living in Martoona forever, had not something strange happened. One day there arrived in the village an old man who had a long white beard and green eyes. He wore bright red shoes turned up at the toes; big, puffy, white silk pantaloons; and an orange silk jacket all embroidered with little gold dragons. Following close behind him was a donkey, snow white in color and with big pink ears. In the top of each ear was a little golden bell that tinkled merrily at every step the donkey took. On its back the donkey carried what seemed to be a huge block of black crystal. At least, that is what it looked like from the one corner that could be seen, for all the rest of it was covered over with a cloth of gold. As the old man went along, he looked neither to the right nor to the left; but he walked straight through the village and did not stop until he came to the inn. By then a great many people—men, women, and children—were walking along behind him; for no one in Martoona had ever seen so strange a sight before. And what was their surprise to see the old man and his donkey go right into the inn, up the stairs, and on into a big room that had a balcony over-looking the main street of Martoona. That was all they saw. Although many of them waited a long time for something to happen, nothing did. At last they went away, still wondering who the old man was, and why he had taken the donkey up to his room with him.

All this happened in the afternoon. By evening every one in the village had heard about the old man and the white donkey with pink ears. Still he remained as much of a mystery as ever. Why he had come, what he wanted, and where he was going, no one knew. There were those, of course, who thought they knew; but they as usual were wrong. And there were those who *said* they knew but weren't allowed to tell. Then there were those who *knew* they didn't know but just wanted to say something. And the more they talked, the more confused they got, until the number of different stories was so great that no one could even count them. And all this just because an old man and a white donkey with pink ears had come to town.

AS THE OLD MAN WENT ALONG, HE LOOKED NEITHER TO THE RIGHT NOR
TO THE LEFT.

B

At supper time word spread through the village that the old man was going to make a speech from the balcony. Most of the people stopped eating right in the middle of supper and ran down the street to the inn. There they gathered in a great crowd under the old man's window. After a time he came out on the balcony, bowed to the crowd, and said:

"My name is Noom-Zor-Noom. I come from the far-off land of Troom. I have heard of Tal, the boy with the golden hair, and have come to see him. Is he here?"

That is all the old man said, nothing else. And the people were disappointed, because they had expected more. What good did it do them to know he came from Troom, when not a person among them knew where Troom was? What did they care about his name, if it meant no more to them than Noom-Zor-Noom? They called and shouted to the old man to make him say more. But he turned his back on them and went to his room. At last the crowd broke up, and the people went home to their half-eaten suppers, which by that time were cold and indigestible.

While all this was going on, Tal was down on the beach digging clams. When he came back to the village, he was not long in finding out what the old man had said. Every one who saw him told him. So he hurried down to the inn, ran up to the old man's room, and knocked at the door.

"Who's there?" asked a deep, kind voice.

"Tal," said the boy.

"Come in," said the old man.

Tal opened the door and walked in. The old man was sitting in a chair near the window. The block of crystal covered with its cloth of gold stood against the wall in one corner of the room. And in one of the beds, all tucked in under the clothes, lay the donkey fast asleep.

"Some one told me you wanted to see me," said Tal. "So I came down as fast as I could."

"I do," said Noom-Zor-Noom. "But we'll have to talk quietly so as not to wake up Millitinkle." He turned and looked at the donkey. "We've come a long way to-day and she's tired. Come over here and sit on my knee, and I'll tell you what I want."

The old man was so kind and so gentle, that Tal never felt the least bit afraid. He was only surprised by everything he saw. A donkey asleep in a bed! He had never seen nor heard of anything like that before. Nor had he ever heard of such a name for a donkey as "Millitinkle." At the same time he could not take his eyes off the old man with his red shoes turned up at the toes, his white pantaloons, his jacket embroidered with gold dragons, and, most of all, his queer green eyes that sparkled and twinkled whenever they looked at the boy. Tal, who only had on a pink sarong and a pair of sandals, felt very much undressed; and he was a little ashamed of himself at first. But when the old man spoke to him a second time, he ran across the room and sat down on his knee.

"Now," said the old man, beginning quietly, "you're Tal, aren't you?"

"Yes," said Tal.

"I'm Noom-Zor-Noom, and I come from the Kingdom of Troom," said the old man. "I've heard all about you. So I've come to see you. I want to take you off on a trip with me. You will see wonderful things and will go to strange lands. But you will always be safe so long as you are in my care. You and Millitinkle and I will travel together. After you have seen and done all you want, I'll bring you back here. So it won't be like going away for good. Would you like to go with me?"

When Tal heard these words that the old man spoke, he did not know what to say. In all his life he had never been outside of Martoona—at least not since he could remember. Nor had he ever thought of such a thing as going on a trip. Yet here was this old man asking him to go. And to go on a trip with a white donkey that had pink ears, and an old man that had green eyes, and a block of black crystal that was covered with a cloth of gold, would certainly be more fun than any other trip in the world. For a moment Tal hung his head and thought. Then he asked, "Where are you going to take me?"

"I can't tell you that until you say you'll come," said Noom-Zor-Noom.

"Have you told any one where you're going to take me?" asked Tal.

"No," said Noom-Zor-Noom.

"What's that thing in the corner?" asked Tal, pointing to the block of crystal.

"I'll tell you if you come," said Noom-Zor-Noom.

Just then there was a tinkling of bells and Millitinkle rolled over in the bed. She opened one eye and looked at Tal. Then she flapped her ears and made the little bells tinkle again. "You'd better come with us," she said. "You'll never have another chance like this."

When Tal heard the donkey speak, he could not believe his ears. "I've never seen a donkey that spoke before," he said. "Does she talk much?"

"Quite a lot," said Noom-Zor-Noom. "But only when she wants to. You can't make her do it, if she doesn't want to."

Everything that Noom-Zor-Noom said, and everything that Tal saw, made him want to go more than ever. So he made up his mind and said, "I'll go with you. When are you leaving?"

"Early to-morrow morning," said Noom-Zor-Noom. "Millitinkle and I shall be leaving here as soon as it's light."

"I'll see you then," said Tal, turning to go.

"All right," said the old man.

So Tal left. He went home. He told the people of Martoona all about what the old man had said: how he wanted to take him on a trip. And the people, when they heard what the boy said, were glad that such a wonderful thing should happen to Tal. The baker gave him some bread; the cobbler made him some new shoes; and every one did everything he could to help him get ready. And that night Tal hardly slept at all, so excited was he at the thought of going off with Noom-Zor-Noom, Millitinkle, and the block of crystal.

CHAPTER II

THE GOLDEN DOOR THAT SPOKE AND WHY
KING TAZZARIN OF TROOM SOUGHT TO OPEN
THE DOOR

THE NEXT MORNING Tal got up before any one else in the village. He put on a brand-new sarong and his new pair of shoes. And in his hand he took a little sack with his few belongings in it. He did not take much, because he was poor and did not have many things. He went out of the house as quietly as he could and ran down to the inn. There he found Noom-Zor-Noom and Milli-tinkle up and ready to start. They had not come downstairs yet, but were still in their room.

"I'm coming with you," said Tal, still out of breath from running so fast. "Now tell me where we are going."

"We are going to Troom," said Noom-Zor-Noom.

"Where's that?" asked Tal.

"You'll find out when we get there," said Noom-Zor-Noom. "It's a long way from here. It's a country all by itself up on a high plateau."

"What's a plateau?" asked Tal.

"An extensive stretch of elevated and comparatively

12

level land," said Millitinkle, flapping her ears and making the little golden bells tinkle.

"I see," said Tal. He really did not. But there was something in the way the donkey spoke that made him ashamed of having asked the question.

"Before we start I want to tell you why I am taking you along," said Noom-Zor-Noom. "I promised you I would last night. After you hear what I have to say, you need not come with me unless you want to."

"I'll want to," said Tal. "I'm sure I shall."

"Then listen to what I have to say," said Noom-Zor-Noom. "And don't ask any questions, because I want to tell you as much as I can before it's time to start." Then the old man made Tal sit down on the side of the bed. And this is what he told him:

"Troom, where I come from, is ruled over by a mighty king called Tazzarin. He has a beautiful palace, and in that palace is a large room with a great throne in it, on which the king sits and rules. The throne is all made out of pure gold, just as a throne should be. In the wall, at one side of the throne, is a huge Golden Door. No one is really sure whether it is a door or not, for it has never been opened. But it looks like a door, so they call it one. This Door is heavy and solid, and right in the middle of it is carved the head of a beautiful woman. As long as any one can remember that woman's head has been there. Each King of Troom knows that when he is in trouble, if he will consult the golden head, it will sometimes speak and give him advice. But always, before the head will speak, a golden plum must be pressed to its lips. If the woman opens her mouth and eats the plum, that means that she is about to speak. If she refuses the plum, then she remains silent. But once she has spoken, her words must be obeyed, or disaster will come to the Kingdom of Troom. This much is known about the Golden Door, and that is all.

"About eight years ago King Tazzarin of Troom had a baby son not more than a year old. The king loved his son more than anything else in the world. And often he would have the little prince brought down to him and put in a cradle at the foot of the throne. Then the king would sit and look and look at his child, he loved him so much. One day while the king had the boy with him, the queen called to him from the next room. The king got down from the throne and went to see what the queen wanted. He left the baby in the cradle, never thinking for a moment that anything would happen. When he came back, the cradle was there, but the baby was gone. The king rushed about the room and called for help. The queen came; the guards came; the menservants and the maidservants came. They looked from one end of the palace to the other, but all in vain. They could find the prince nowhere; nor could they see a sign of any kind that told where the baby had gone.

"The king was beside himself with grief. And when he was sure that nothing he could do would bring back

THE KING LOVED HIS SON MORE THAN ANYTHING ELSE IN THE WORLD.
AND OFTEN HE WOULD HAVE THE LITTLE PRINCE BROUGHT DOWN TO HIM
AND PUT IN A CRADLE AT THE FOOT OF THE THRONE.

his son, he made up his mind to consult the Golden Door. So that night he called together the wise men of Troom and said, 'This and that has happened to my son. Nothing that I can do will bring him back or even find where he has gone. So I am going to consult the Golden Door.'

"When the wise men heard the words that the king spoke they shook their heads and said, 'It is better to wait a little longer. If we consult the woman's head, we shall have to obey her words, or disaster will come to the kingdom. She may command such things as are not within our power to do. It is much better to wait. No king before you has ever consulted the Door so readily.'

"The king said, 'There can be no greater disaster than to have the prince stolen. What could happen that would be worse? Tell me, and I will do as you say.'

"The wise men could not tell him. So the king made ready to consult the Door. He called for a golden plum. And when it was brought to him, he pressed it to the woman's lips. At once her lips became as if alive, and she ate the plum. Then she said, 'O king, your son has been carried off by a djinn. He is safe, but he will not come back to you until a story is told that pleases the Golden Door. It must be such a story as a child would love. To-morrow night five stories are to be told in this room, one by each of the five best story-tellers in Troom. If the Door does not open, in another year five more stories are to be told; and so on, year after year. When the right story shall be told, then the Golden Door will open, and your son will come back. But until that time, no power on earth can bring back the prince.' After that the head said nothing more. It stopped talking, and all was silent.

"The king said, 'Her words are easy to obey. It is good that I have consulted her. She must mean that the prince is behind the Door. It would be well to open it by force and see.'

"The wise men shook their heads and said, 'Do not touch the Door. It has always been shut. Let it remain so. Terrible things might happen if we opened it.'

"The king said, 'I must see if my son is behind it.' He paid no attention to what the wise men advised. Instead, he called the soldiers of his guard and ordered them to batter the Door down at once. But all the battering and all the strength of the men did not budge the Door a single inch. They tried everything they could, but the Door would not open; nor could they harm the head of the woman that was carved on it. So King Tazzarin ordered his men off and left the Door as it was.

"From the day that his child was taken away King Tazzarin became a cruel and hard ruler. All he could do was mourn for the lost prince, and he paid little or no attention to the needs of the people of Troom. He proclaimed an order that no child should come into or go out of the kingdom until his own son was found.

Every year he picked five men who each told a story in front of the Golden Door. And when these men failed to open the Door, they were seized, put in chains, and thrown into prison. For eight years the Door has remained shut. Forty different men have tried stories and failed. And the people of Troom, as well as King Tazzarin himself, are beginning to think that no one will ever open the Door. Time after time they have tried to make the woman speak. But she remains silent and will not eat the golden plums that are pressed to her lips. So the king can do nothing but keep on having stories told every year in hopes that some day he may see his son again.

"This year," said Noom-Zor-Noom, "I have been chosen as one of the story-tellers. For many months I have been traveling all over the world, gathering as many stories as possible. Now it is nearly time for me to be back in Troom. I have heard about you, Tal, and I think that a story that would please you might please the Golden Door. So I want you to travel back to Troom with me, and on the way I shall tell you such stories as I have. If you hear them all and tell me which one you like best, there may be some chance of my opening the Door. If I don't open the Door, I must go to prison."

Tal listened to everything the old man had to say. And, of course, the more he heard, the more he wanted to go to the Kingdom of Troom. He said, "I'd love to go with you and hear your stories. But I'd hate to have you go to prison because I chose the wrong one. What makes you think that my choice will be any better than any one else's?"

"I know it will," said Noom-Zor-Noom. "Any child would love a story that pleased a boy like you."

For a moment Tal was silent, then he said, "What are you going to do with me when we get to Troom? Don't you think that King Tazzarin might let me in? *You* ask him if he won't!"

"We'll see about that when we get there," said Noom-Zor-Noom. "Are you sure that you want to go?"

"Of course I am," said Tal. "I wouldn't miss such a trip for anything."

By then it was getting light outside; the day was breaking. Noom-Zor-Noom walked to the corner of the room, and with a great deal of trouble and care he lifted the block of crystal up and strapped it on to Millitinkle's back. Then he said to Tal, "Come on, now. We must be going. We have a long way ahead of us." The three of them left the room and went down the stairs, first Noom-Zor-Noom, then Tal, and then Millitinkle. When they came out into the street, they found that all the people of Martoona had come to say good-bye to Tal. They were standing in a great crowd around the door of the inn. Some of them looked happy, but most of them were sad at the thought of parting with the boy. Noom-Zor-Noom, who saw things as they were, turned to them and said, "I will not keep Tal with me long. He shall come back safely to you. While he is with me he will see such things as no child has ever seen before.

He has been good and has worked hard and deserves a trip."

The people, when they heard what the old man said and how nicely he said it, did not feel at all worried about Tal. They were glad that he was going to see such things. So they all shouted good-bye to him and told him to come back soon. While this was going on, Noom-Zor-Noom reached under the cloth that covered the crystal block and pulled out a bag. The next minute he was throwing handful after handful of gold pieces to the people. While they were all busy looking at the ground and picking up pieces of gold, Tal and Noom-Zor-Noom and Millitinkle disappeared: they were not to be seen any more. None of the people of Martoona saw in what direction they went. All they knew was that the last any one saw of Tal he was walking down the street with the old man with green eyes and the white, pink-eared donkey that carried a block of crystal on her back.

C

CHAPTER III

THE BLACK CRYSTAL BLOCK AND THE STORY
OF THE ENCHANTED TAPESTRY

THE ROAD that Tal, Noom-Zor-Noom, and Millitinkle took led up the side of a steep mountain. All morning they went along it. They saw nothing, only rocks and trees, and far, far below them the shining sea.

At first Noom-Zor-Noom was rather quiet. But when they had gone a good distance and were well away from Martoona, he began to talk and ask Tal many questions about his life. And Tal, in turn, asked him about where they were going and what they were going to see. In this way they walked on side by side, chatting and talking for all they were worth. Millitinkle followed behind without saying a word. But by the way she pricked up her ears and turned them forward and made the little bells tinkle, it was quite clear that she missed nothing of what was being said.

At last, after they had climbed for many hours, they came to a great wall of snow and ice. The wall was so high that not even the tallest man in the world could look over the top. And in the wall there was a gate where the road went through. Here Noom-Zor-Noom stopped and said to Tal, "Before we go any further, you must have a coat; because it will be cold on the other side of the wall." He reached under the golden cloth that covered the crystal block and pulled out a white fur coat that was exactly the right size for the boy. Tal put it on; and when he felt how warm it was, he said, "I'll be warm enough. But how about Millitinkle?"

"Don't worry about her," said the old man. "Watch and see what happens to her, when she goes through the gate. And when we get on the other side of the wall, don't be afraid of what you see. Stay close to me. Nothing will harm you."

After the old man had spoken, they started to go through the gate. As they went, Millitinkle's fur grew longer and longer, until, by the time they had passed through, she had fur as long and as thick as that worn by a polar bear. So Tal did not have to worry about her being cold.

On the other side of the wall they found themselves in a country that was all white. As they were going along the road, a white leopard sprang out from behind a white rock and roared and asked, "Who are you, and why do you come to my country?"

Noom-Zor-Noom said, "I am on my way back to Troom, where I live."

The leopard said, "It is my business to stop people from going to Troom. That's what I'm here for. How am I to know you really live there?"

When the leopard spoke these words, Noom-Zor-

Noom took out his two green eyes and handed them to the animal.

The leopard asked, "What color?"

Noom-Zor-Noom said, "Red."

So the leopard bounded off and went back behind his rock, where he had a lot of eyes of many different colors. He picked out a pair of red ones and brought them back to the old man. The old man took the eyes and put them in his head: they fitted exactly. When the leopard saw that the eyes belonged to the old man, he said nothing more. He went back to his rock and let Noom-Zor-Noom, Millitinkle, and Tal go on their way.

After they had left the leopard a good way behind, Tal said to Noom-Zor-Noom, "Why did you give that leopard your eyes? Mine don't come out that way."

"I had to do it," said the old man. "Otherwise he would not have let us pass."

"But didn't it hurt?" asked Tal.

"No," said the old man. "My eyes are made to come out."

Millitinkle flapped her ears; the little golden bells tinkled; and she said, "If your eyes were made to come out, it wouldn't hurt to take them out."

"Probably not," said Tal. "But mine aren't made that way."

"That doesn't mean some one else's can't be," said the donkey. "Wouldn't it be awful if we were all the same?"

"It would," said Tal. "I hadn't thought of it that way."

"It's a lot to think about," said Millitinkle, and she spoke no more.

All that afternoon they walked through the white country. They saw no villages, no houses, no people of any kind. But they did see many animals. White bears, white wolves, white tigers, and white lions came to the side of the road and watched them pass. And Tal wondered at these animals, for he had never seen such tame animals before. He wanted to stop and talk with them; but Noom-Zor-Noom would not let him, saying that they had far to go and must get to the other side of the country before night. So they walked on and on, without once stopping to rest or eat.

Just at evening they came again to a wall with a gate in it. And near the gate there was an inn. Here they stopped for the night. The inn was owned by a white horse. And when the horse saw Noom-Zor-Noom, he came out from the inn and greeted him, saying, "You have been gone a long time. Did you find the stories you wanted?"

Noom-Zor-Noom said, "I have heard many stories. And I am bringing Tal with me that he may hear them. The one he likes best, I shall tell."

When Tal heard what Noom-Zor-Noom said to the horse, he was proud. He stood up straight and held his hands by his side and smiled with the corners of his mouth.   Then the horse stepped over and shook hands with him.   After that they all went into the inn and had supper.

Now this horse knew all about the Golden Door, for Noom-Zor-Noom had told him when he stayed at the inn many months before.   In the meanwhile the horse had been waiting for the old man to come back.   And he was happy to see him again.   He asked him many questions about where he had been and what he had seen.   And Noom-Zor-Noom told him all.   Then the horse asked, "Do you think you will be able to open the Golden Door?"

Noom-Zor-Noom said, "That I do not know.   I have many stories.   One of them should please the Door.   If not, I shall have to go to prison and spend the rest of my life in chains.   King Tazzarin will have no mercy."

At these words the horse felt sad.   He did not want his friend to go to prison.   He said, "Tell us one of your stories.   If it is good, I shall tell you so.   If not, you will know that it has not pleased me."

And Tal said, "Please tell us one.   If I don't like it, I'll say so."

Noom-Zor-Noom got up and went over to the side of the room where the block of black crystal was.   He lifted it up and carried it over and set it down on the table.   Then he took off the cloth that covered it.   When he did this, Tal saw that all one side of the block was covered with many lines of small writing. It was so small that Tal could not read it. Even if he could, it would have done him no good; for it was in a language he did not understand. Just the same, he wondered what it was. He asked, "What's all that writing on the top of the block?"

Noom-Zor-Noom said, "Everywhere, when I heard a good story, I wrote it down in golden letters on this block. These are the stories from which you must choose. Before we get to Troom you will have heard them all."

Tal asked, "But what did you write them down with?"

Noom-Zor-Noom said, "With gold paint."

"You haven't got any gold paint with you," said Tal. "Where is it?"

Then Noom-Zor-Noom slid out one end of the crystal block and showed Tal how it was all hollow inside. He reached in and took out a jug of gold paint and a little brush. While he was doing this, Tal peeped in and saw a silver wand and a golden ball. That was all he had time to see before the old man slid back the end and closed it up. Then he held up the jug and brush and said, " I write with these."

Tal asked, "What language do you write in?"

"In a language that only I can read," said Noom-Zor-Noom.

"Why do you do that?" asked Tal.

Then Millitinkle, who had been talking with the horse, turned around and said, "Why shouldn't he?"

"I don't know," said Tal. "That isn't what I asked. I want to know why he should."

"Because there's no reason why he shouldn't," said the donkey. "That's why he does it."

"Then the only reason for doing anything is because there's no reason why you shouldn't," said Tal. "Is that what you mean?"

"Exactly," said the donkey.

"Not always," said Noom-Zor-Noom. "Sometimes there's a very good reason why you should. And the reason is that I didn't want any one else to be able to read these stories. I want them all to myself."

"That's what I thought," said Tal.

"Then why did you ask?" said Millitinkle.

"Because I wasn't sure," said Tal. "And I wanted to find out."

After that the donkey said nothing more. Noom-Zor-Noom carefully put the jug and the brush back inside the crystal block in such a way that Tal did not have a chance to look in again. Then Tal, Millitinkle, and the horse all sat down around the table, while Noom-Zor-Noom read one of his stories. He read them the first one, the one right up at the top of the crystal block. The story was called

THE ENCHANTED TAPESTRY

FAR AWAY, in a country that was all mountains, there lived a beautiful princess named Azure. Like all the rest of the people who lived in that country Azure lived on the top of a mountain. But the mountain that she lived on was different from the other mountains. In the first place it was much higher than any of the rest. Then, instead of being made of rocks and snow like most mountains, it was all made of silver. Of course, it was very, very pretty, and it shone and sparkled in the sunlight. But its sides were so polished and so slippery that no one could go either up or down them.

Azure had lived on the mountain as long as she could remember. None of the other people knew how she got there. Often they would see her walking around the top of the mountain, but that was all they knew about her. Even Azure did not know who brought her there. The most she knew was that when she was a baby a great bird had come and picked her out of her cradle. That was all she remembered. So, of course, she thought that the bird had carried her off and left her on the mountain top.

Up where Azure lived things were different from any place else in the world. It was always warm and sunny, and it never rained. On this account she did not need a house, for she could always live out in the fields and the

woods. When night came, she did not have to be afraid
of anything, she just lay down in a cave, or under a tree,
or on the grass, and went to sleep.

The trees were not like our trees: they were all made
of crystal with emerald leaves. The fruit they bore was
of precious stones—rubies, diamonds, sapphires, and
many other kinds. And the grass itself was not green
but a beautiful yellow, because it was all thin blades of
gold. Even the flowers were made of many, many
jewels of different colors, and they grew on silver stems.

In the midst of all this beauty Azure lived alone. She
had no friend to play with and no one to talk to. She
did not even have the fun of eating, for she was never
hungry. Of course she grew like any other person, but
she did not have to eat to do it. Often, after she had been
playing all day, Azure would be lonely. When she was
that way, she used to go and sit by the edge of a lovely
mountain pool. There she would sit for hours, gazing
into the depths of the clear water and wishing she had
some one to play with.

One day when she was looking into the water she saw,
far down in the deepest part of the pool, a pair of hands.
They were not nice-looking hands, for they were too
large, and the fingers were long and bony. Just the
same, they were some one's hands; and this amazed
Azure, who could not understand how any one could
live at the bottom of a pool. She looked at them so
hard and put her face so close to the water that she almost

fell in. But she could see nothing more than just the hands.

That night Azure hardly slept at all. All she could think of was the hands in the bottom of the pool. All she wanted to do was to run back and look at them again, but she could not see them in the dark. As soon as the sun came up, Azure ran to the pool, and there were the hands. But this time, instead of being empty, they were holding a large piece of tapestry. This surprised Azure very much. And she was more surprised when she saw the hands pick up a golden needle and start to work on the tapestry. They worked nimbly and with the greatest care, making each stitch as nearly perfect as possible. Azure watched until her eyes could see no more; then she went to sleep sitting right there on the edge of the pool.

After this, every day, all day long, Azure did nothing but look at the tapestry. Of course, it grew very slowly, for the workmanship was of the finest kind. But it did grow, and the first thing to be finished was the figure of a young prince. He had red hair and blue eyes, and he wore a sword at his side. Azure no sooner saw him, than she wanted him for a friend. It would be so nice to have some one to play with. And the prince was just the person she wanted. But it did her no good, for *he* was at the bottom of the pool; and *she* had no way of going down to get him.

One morning, when Azure went to the pool, she saw

that the water was bubbling and boiling as if a fire had been lighted underneath it. She could not understand this at all, because until then the water had always been so calm. She looked down into it and, at first, could see nothing. Then she caught a glimpse of one of the hands. It was moving and flying about as if struggling with something. The faster it moved, the more the water stirred and seethed. So Azure knew that a terrible struggle was going on down below. And she was sure that she would never see her prince again. Hard as she looked, she could make nothing out at all clearly. This broke her heart, and she sat down and began to cry. She had about given up all hope of ever seeing the prince, when all of a sudden the tapestry, with the golden needle sticking in one corner, floated to the surface of the pool. After it came a lot of threads. At once, without even taking off her clothes, Azure jumped into the water, grabbed the tapestry and threads, and swam back to shore with them.

After she had dried her clothes and the tapestry by hanging them on a crystal tree, she got dressed and sat down to look at the prince. She thought how nice it would be if he were only alive. She touched him and spoke to him, but he never said a word. She even pinched him to see if he would squeal. And when he did not, she pinched him harder and harder, but not a sound came out of him. So she made up her mind that he was not much of a playmate after all.

Azure, of course, was bitterly disappointed to find that

the prince was not alive. So, for want of anything better to do, she made up her mind to finish the tapestry. Day after day she worked on it, until her fingers grew sore. First she put in a stream, then a pond, then a castle, then some woods, then a wild boar, and finally a lot of hunters and many other people. Every figure she made, she tried to do just as beautifully as the prince was done. In this way she spent a great deal of time and was quite happy.

After a year of constant work, she at last finished all except a small piece in one corner. This piece she hated to do, for she knew that once the tapestry was finished she would have nothing else to pass the time with. So she took only one stitch every day. At this rate she went on until but one stitch was left. Then she thought to herself, "I shall take the tapestry to my favorite spot and there finish it." She picked everything up and went to the side of a stream that ran through a wooded dell. There she sat down on her favorite rock, took the golden needle, and pulled the last bit of thread through the tapestry. As she pulled it tight, what was her surprise to see the prince step out and sit down on the rock beside her. Azure was too excited to say anything. She sat in silence and gazed at her little friend.

"You have saved me," said the prince. "Now I will give you whatever you wish."

"But who are you?" Azure asked, still too surprised to know what had happened.

"I am Bamba," said the prince.

"How did you get in the tapestry?" asked Azure.

Then Bamba told her that a terrible ogress lived inside the mountain, and that this ogress was in the habit of stealing children and sewing them into tapestries.

"What made the ogress let you go?" asked Azure, who could hardly believe what she heard.

"It must have been my father who came and killed her," said Bamba. "I can't think of anything else."

After they had talked for a while, and Bamba had told all about what happened to him, he asked Azure how she got on the mountain top. And all that Azure could tell him was about the bird. When Bamba heard this story, he knew at once that Azure was his sister, for his father had often told him how she had been stolen by a bird. So they kissed each other and were very happy.

The first thing in the mind of each of them was how they could get back to their home. Azure was so excited that she was not of much use in thinking up a plan. But Bamba knew at once what to do. He had Azure lead him to the woods, and there with his sword he cut down a crystal tree. After he had taken all the branches off, he made out of the trunk a sled that was just big enough to hold them both. Then he picked two diamond pears and put them on the front of the sled for lights. By the time this was done, the day was nearly over. So, dragging their sled behind them, they hurried to the edge of the mountain. There they stopped, while

AND OFF THEY WENT DOWN THE SIDE OF THE SILVER MOUNTAIN.

Bamba showed Azure how she was to sit in the front of the sled and hold on with all her might. She did as he told her. Then Bamba gave the sled a push from behind and jumped on. And off they went down the side of the silver mountain. Faster and faster they went. The wind whistled by their faces and blew Azure's hair far out behind her. The diamond pears shone like two very bright stars and lit up the mountainside for a great distance around. All that night they coasted and all the next day. Not once did they stop, but always they went down, down, and down. At last, when the day was almost over, they came to the foot of the mountain. There they spent the night in a cave that Bamba knew about. They hid the sled away where they could find it again and set out to climb the mountain on which their own home was. Their father and mother could not believe their eyes when they saw them coming. They welcomed them and showed great joy to have them back again. Then Azure told her story and Bamba told his. And after they were both done, their father told how he had slain the terrible ogress that stole children. That night Azure and Bamba had everything they liked best for supper. They stayed with their parents and have lived happily ever since.

WHEN Noom-Zor-Noom finished the story, he asked what they thought of it. The horse was so pleased that he could not say enough in its praise. And Tal, who had

D

been listening to every word, begged Noom-Zor-Noom
to go on and read another. But the old man was tired.
He put the golden cloth back over the crystal block and
said, "There is not time for another to-night. We must
go to bed now, for we have to be up early in the
morning."

Millitinkle flapped her ears; the little bells tinkled;
and she said, "I'm not going to bed. I'm going to sit
up and talk with the horse. I haven't seen him for a
long time, and I have many things to tell him."

"All right," said the old man, "do as you wish. But
Tal has got to go to bed."

So Millitinkle stayed downstairs. The horse showed
Noom-Zor-Noom and Tal to their room. They went to
bed and slept that night at the inn.

CHAPTER IV

THE SILVER BOAT AND THE STORY OF THE TURTLE

THE NEXT MORNING Tal, Noom-Zor-Noom, and Millitinkle were up early. They ate breakfast, said good-bye
to the horse, and left the inn. They went out through
the gate in the wall; and, as they went out, Millitinkle's
hair grew short again. She shook herself and said,
"That feels better. I don't like long hair."

"Neither should I," said Tal. Then, without thinking, he went on and said, "It must be an awful nuisance
to have hair all over you. It's bad enough just having
it on your head."

"What!" said Millitinkle.

"I mean it must be awfully hard to comb it and brush
it," said Tal, afraid that he had hurt the donkey's feelings. "But you take care of yours beautifully."

"That's not what you said at first," answered Millitinkle. "You said that you thought it would be awful
to have hair all over your body. I'll show you whether
it is or not." And before Tal could even answer her,
she stretched out her neck, brayed three times, and all
her hair disappeared. There she stood in the middle of
the road with nothing on but her pink skin.

"I didn't mean what I said," cried Tal. "I'm sorry.

39

I hate you that way." But Millitinkle paid no attention. She just stood there as she was. Then Tal began to cry, for he felt that he had said the wrong thing. He looked up at Noom-Zor-Noom and said, "Please make her grow it back. I didn't mean what I said."

"I know you didn't," answered the old man. "But you said it just the same."

"But I wasn't thinking," said Tal.

"You should have been," said Noom-Zor-Noom. "I'm sure she will forgive you this time. Hereafter you must be careful, for there's no telling how Millitinkle will take what you say. I'll see what she wants to do." He walked over and whispered something in her ear. Then Millitinkle wagged her tail and brayed three times more, and her hair came back. For a time she was stubborn and cross and kept looking at Tal with a queer, insulted look. But after a while she forgave him, and they were just as good friends as before.

They went on their way and followed the road down the side of a steep mountain. Though it kept getting warmer and warmer, Tal did not dare say anything about taking off his coat, for fear of what Millitinkle might think. Near the bottom of the mountain they came to a big forest. Through the middle of this the road went; and the shade of the trees felt good to Tal. At last they came to a river. The river was wide, much wider than any river Tal had ever seen. And there was no bridge across it, nor was there any boat in sight. But right where the road came to the bank of the river there was a big round bowlder about twelve feet high. And on top of this bowlder sat an elephant, fast asleep.

This elephant was the ferryman. It was his task to take people across the river. Whoever wanted to go across had to stand on top of the bowlder, while the elephant rolled it through the water. The bowlder was so high that the top of it was always out of water. This was the only way to get across, there was no other.

This elephant was kind. He was also wise. He used to charge a peanut apiece for taking people across. In this way he got his food, enough to live on poorly. But what he loved most of all was to ask riddles. And any one who answered his riddle, that person he took across without pay.

Noom-Zor-Noom shouted to the elephant and said, "Wake up! We want to cross the river."

The elephant flapped one ear, opened one eye, and said, "Who are you and what do you want?" And he went to sleep again and began to snore.

"We want to cross the river," said Noom-Zor-Noom. "Get down from the bowlder and take us across!"

The elephant only snored louder. He was so fast asleep that he lost his balance, slid off the rock, and landed in the water with a splash. Then he made a great fuss. He trumpeted and asked, "Who pushed me off the rock?"

"No one," said Noom-Zor-Noom. "You fell off yourself. If you'd waked up when I spoke to you, it wouldn't have happened."

"Some one pushed me off," said the elephant. "I couldn't fall without being pushed."

"Yes, you could," said Millitinkle.

"No, I couldn't," said the elephant.

"Yes, you could."

"No, I couldn't."

"Yes, you could."

"No, I couldn't."

"Yes, you could—could—could—could—coulD—couLD—coULD—cOULD—COULD!" said Millitinkle in such quick succession that the elephant did not have time to answer her. So he said nothing more; for what was the use of arguing with a donkey?

"We want to get to the other side of the river," said Noom-Zor-Noom. "Will you take us?"

"I will," said the elephant. "But first I must ask you a riddle. Tell me: Why do I push this bowlder back and forth across the river?"

Noom-Zor-Noom thought and said, "Because it won't go by itself."

"No. That's not the answer," said the elephant.

"I know," said Tal. "Because you're bold, but the bowlder's bowlder."

The elephant winked at Tal and said, "That might be the reason. But it's not the one I'm thinking of. Just the same it was a good guess. You'll have to pay only half a peanut."

Then Millitinkle looked very wise. She flapped her

THIS ELEPHANT WAS THE FERRYMAN.

ears; the little bells tinkled; and she said, "Because you can't carry it in your trunk."

"That's right," said the elephant. "You get a free ride."

After that Noom-Zor-Noom gave the elephant a peanut and a half. And he took them across the river one at a time. First he lifted Millitinkle up and put her on the top of the bowlder and pushed her across. Then Noom-Zor-Noom went. And last of all went Tal. He found it easy to ride on top of the bowlder, because the elephant rolled it so slowly. At the other side of the river they gave the elephant another peanut, because they had waked him up. Then they thanked him and went their way.

The road that they took still led them through the woods. They followed it as far as it went; and it took them to the shore of the sea. There the road ended; it went no further.

"The boat's not here yet," said Noom-Zor-Noom, looking up and down the beach. "It's usually tied to that big flat rock over there. That's the only place where the water is deep enough for it to come in."

"Where are we going in the boat?" asked Tal.

"We have to cross the sea to get to Troom," said Noom-Zor-Noom. "I don't know how we'd get across unless we went in a boat."

"Is it too far to swim?" asked Tal.

Noom-Zor-Noom laughed and said, "It's thousands of miles. Even now we can only get there in time by taking the fastest boat there is. It will be here before long. While we wait, I'll read you another story."

"How long do you think we'll have to wait?" asked Tal. "Where is the boat coming from?"

Noom-Zor-Noom did not hear his question. He was busy lifting the crystal block off Millitinkle's back. He set it down on the sand and made ready to read. While he was doing this, Millitinkle trotted off and went swimming. She brayed and splashed and made so much noise, that Noom-Zor-Noom could not start his story until she was done. After she had come out of the water and was sitting on the sand, the old man started to read the story of

THE TURTLE

IN A LAKE on the top of a hill there lived a big turtle. The turtle had always been in the lake as long as any one could remember, but no one had ever seen him close to. From a distance he looked like any other turtle, except

that he was many times bigger and 𝟷
silver. So smooth and so highly polisʜ.
that it reflected the sunlight just like a mirrᴏ.
reason the turtle could be seen even when he wᴀ.
down in the water. Perhaps this had something to ᴏᴜ
with the story that grew up about the turtle. Whether
it did or not, the story was that a wish would be granted
to any one who could get close enough to see his own
image in the turtle's shell. All the people who lived at
the bottom of the hill believed this. And, though none
of them had ever had a chance to look, yet they always
hoped they would. Therefore they treated the turtle
kindly, threw food to him often, and thought of him
almost as a sacred animal.

In the village at the bottom of the hill the people grew
flowers: that was all they did. In this way they made
their living; and it was a good living, for nowhere else
in the whole kingdom did such beautiful flowers grow.
And the reason they were so beautiful was that the people
knew a certain secret about growing flowers which they
had never told to any one else. Therefore, this secret
was only known to those people who lived at the bottom
of that hill on the top of which, in a lake, lived the turtle
with the silver shell.

There, in that village, lived a boy and a girl who were
brother and sister. The girl's name was Teteena; and
the boy was called Jath, which is short for Jathemmar-
radal. Though Teteena was many years younger than
her brother, he and she were just as good friends as if

they had been the same age. They always went around together; they always played together; and they always worked together in their gardens. They often talked about what they would do when they grew up: how they would live together and have a garden more beautiful than any other garden in the village. They never thought that the time might come when they would be separated. And probably it never would have, had not something terrible happened.

One day the king came to this village. And when he saw the beautiful flowers, he thought to himself, "I have no such flowers as these in my own gardens. It would be well if I knew the secret of how to grow them." So he started to ask questions. And the more questions he asked, the less he found out; for the people had no idea of giving away their secret, not even to the king. At last the king grew angry and said, "Will you tell me your secret, or will you not?"

The people said, "If we tell you our secret, the charm will be broken. So it will do you no good, nor will it any longer be of use to us."

When the king heard what they had to say, he did not believe them. He said, "Very well; then keep your secret! But I will find out for myself. I will take a boy from this village back with me. And he can teach my gardeners how to grow flowers. If he refuses to teach them, I'll put him in prison and send for another boy. In this way I'll find out your secret. You might just as well tell me now, it will be much better for you."

But nothing that the king said made any difference to the people. Finally he did what he had threatened to do. He ordered all the boys of the village to be sent before him, and from them he picked one to take back to the palace. Though the people shouted, "It will do you no good, he will not give away the secret"; the king paid no attention. He only said, "If he will not teach my gardeners the secret, then he will go to prison." With these words, he and his followers went off with the boy. And the boy was Jath, the brother of Teteena.

After Jath had been taken away, Teteena did nothing but cry. She lost all interest in everything: she did not even wish to eat. Day after day she sat in her garden, cried softly to herself, and wondered what she could do to get her brother back. She thought, "He will never give away the secret. He will be put into prison, and I'll never see him again. There must be something I can do to help him." And the more she thought, the harder she cried, until it seemed that there could not possibly be any more tears left in her eyes.

A month passed, and not a word was heard from Jath. One afternoon, while Teteena was sitting in her garden, a storm blew up. For an hour the rain fell with great force. Then the skies cleared, and in the east appeared a beautiful rainbow. It was very big and very broad, and it looked as if it began somewhere up near the lake where the turtle lived. Teteena looked at it and said to herself, "I have never seen such a rainbow! It must begin up there in the lake. I'll run up. Maybe I can see!" Without another thought she was off and up the hillside. When she reached the top of the hill, she saw the rainbow rising right out of the middle of the lake. While she stood on the shore gazing at it, the turtle with the silver shell crawled out of the water almost at her feet. Teteena did not miss the chance. She looked into the silver shell, saw her own image, and wished that Jath would come back. And no sooner had she made her wish, than the turtle slid back into the water and swam away.

Teteena stood where she was, wondering what was going to happen now that she had looked into the shell. Before long she saw the turtle come to the surface in the middle of the lake, pick up the end of the rainbow on his back, and start swimming to shore with it. As he came nearer and nearer, Teteena was seized with a great desire to jump on to his back: that was all she wanted to do. So she took off her shoes and stockings; and, as soon as the turtle came near enough, she gave a jump and landed on his back. The next minute she was walking up the rainbow just as you or I would walk over a bridge. At first all the bright colors dazzled her. But her eyes soon grew used to them. Then she saw that the rainbow was made out of millions and millions of little sparkling jewels. Up and up she went, until she came to the top. There she stopped for a minute to rest and catch her breath. After that, without once thinking what might happen to her, she sat down and began to slide down the other side. The wind whistled and shrieked and blew in her face; and changing colors streaked before her eyes. Still she kept on going down. And all the time she had a queer feeling that she was getting smaller and smaller. At last she began to slow up. When she looked to see what had happened to her, she saw that she had shrunk into a little yellow person with little yellow wings on her ankles. Just before she came to the end of the rainbow, she gave a jump, flew off into the air, and fluttered down in the center of a crowd of tiny people who were all different colors and also had wings on their ankles the same as hers.

"Who are you?" she asked, for she was surprised and had no idea where she was.

"Tell us who you are first; then we'll tell you who we are," they said.

So Teteena told them all about her brother and about the turtle and about the way she had come over the rainbow. Then she said, "You must tell me who you are. Where am I?"

They said, "We are the people who give colors to things. We live on this side of the rainbow. It is our task to see that all of the flowers have colors."

She said, "You mean you paint all the flowers?"

"Exactly," they said. "We go about in the night with little paint buckets and brushes. Those of us who are blue paint the blue flowers. Those of us who are red paint the red flowers. Those of us who are white paint the white flowers. Because you are yellow, you shall have to take care of the yellow flowers."

"I didn't come here to paint flowers," said Teteena, for she did not see that this had anything to do with her wish. "I came here to get Jath back."

"We know that," they said. "But while you are with us, you'll have to work."

"Will I have to paint yellow flowers all alone?" she asked. "I've never painted in my life."

"No," they said. "There are lots of other Yellows to help you. They'll teach you what to do. From now on your name is Yellow Ten-Million-Four-Hundred-And-Twenty-Three-Thousand-Two-Hundred-And-One."

"That can't be right," she said. "My *real* name is Teteena. I can't have two names."

"Yes, you can," they said. "As long as you are with us it's Yellow Ten-Million-Four-Hundred-And-Twenty-Three-Thousand-Two-Hundred-And-One."

"I can't remember that," said Teteena. "It's much too long. Teteena is the only name I've ever had. Can't I keep it?"

"No," they said. "Not if you wish to stay with us."

"Then tell me my name again, and I'll try to remember it," she said.

"This is the short way of saying it," they said. "Y-One-Zero-Four-Two-Three-Two-Zero-One."

"Y-One-Zero-Four . . ." said Teteena, and she could not remember any more.

". . . Two-Three-Two-Zero-One," said the people, finishing it up for her. "Yours is a short name. Lots of them are longer."

After Teteena had repeated it correctly several times out loud, she asked, "Now what am I to do?"

"You are to fly over there," they said, all pointing to a big field of buttercups. "The other Yellows are at work now coloring those buttercups. You go and help them."

So Teteena, still muttering her new name to herself, flew over to where they pointed. There she found thousands and thousands of yellow people just like herself. They were hard at work painting the buttercups. One of them gave her a small brush and a pot of paint and showed her what to do. She worked for a while, and then she said, "I thought you painted the flowers at night."

"We do," said one of the Yellows. "But first we learn how to paint here. After you've learned, you'll be sent to a real garden. You will have to take care of it every night."

So Teteena set to work and learned how to paint yellow flowers: first buttercups, then tulips, then primroses, then sunflowers, then roses, and then every other kind of yellow flower that there was. She learned so well, that she could paint them better than any of the little

E

yellow people that she worked with. Finally the queen of all the Flower Painters sent for her and said, "You have worked hard and have learned well. Now I am going to send you to a real garden. Where would you like to go?"

"To the king's garden," said Teteena. "And if you'll send the best painters along with me, maybe I can make that garden so beautiful that the king will let Jath come home."

"That's just what I was going to tell you to do," said the queen. "You can take any of the painters you wish."

Teteena thanked the queen for what she had said. She went off and picked out the best painters of every color. And together they flew off that night to the garden of the king. There they worked night after night, until the flowers in the garden became almost as beautiful as those that grew in the village at the bottom of the hill. But all the time that Teteena was there, she never saw her brother, nor did she hear a word about him.

After she had worked in the garden for a long time, Teteena went to the queen and said, "I have done all I can do, and I have not once seen my brother. There is no use of my working any more. I'd like to go home." And she was very sad, for she really thought her brother had gone away for good.

The queen said, "You can go. But don't be sad. I think that everything will be all right."

"It can't be," said Teteena. "I know that Jath will never tell the secret. So he must be in prison. That's why I didn't see him."

"But you were only in the garden at night," said the queen. "That's why you didn't see him. He was in bed, asleep."

"One day," said Teteena, "I stayed in the garden all day and hid under a big leaf. Even then I didn't see Jath. I saw the other gardeners, but not Jath."

"He may not have worked that day," said the queen, trying to cheer up Teteena. "Anyhow, don't be sad. You go back home and see what has happened."

"How will I get there?" asked Teteena.

"The same way as you came," said the queen. With these words, she took Teteena by the hand and flew with her over to the end of the rainbow. There she said, "You walk up this side and slide down the other. Then you'll turn back to yourself again." She kissed the girl good-bye and sent her off up the rainbow.

Teteena did as the queen told her. She walked up the rainbow, and when she came to the top she sat down and slid down the other side. By the time she reached the bottom, she was her own size again, just as she had been before she crossed over the rainbow. She stepped off on to the turtle's shell; and he carried her to shore. She looked about for her shoes and stockings, but they were not there. So she hurried down the hillside and home as fast as she could with bare feet.

When she came to her house, there was Jath waiting to greet her. He said, "What happened to you? Where have you been? We found your shoes and stockings up by the lake, and we were afraid that you had been drowned."

Teteena told him what had happened to her. But she did not say that she had been painting flowers in the king's garden. After she had finished her story, she said to her brother, "How is it that you have come back? Did you give away the secret?"

"No," said Jath. "I wouldn't tell the secret. So the king put me in prison. After I had been there for a while, he came to me one day and said, 'My gardeners must have learned your secret. Never before have there been such wonderful flowers. You may go home. I do not need you any more.' And before I had time to say that I hadn't given away the secret, the king took me out of prison and sent me home."

"And you really hadn't given it away at all?" asked Teteena.

"No," said Jath.

Then Teteena told him how she had gone and painted the flowers in the king's garden. And Jath said, "You saved my life. What can I do for you?"

"Stay with me all the time," said Teteena, "and never, never go away."

So Jath and Teteena lived together and had their garden just as they planned. But every year, on the same day, Teteena had to go over the rainbow and stay with the Flower Painters long enough to paint the king's garden. In this way the people who lived in the village at the bottom of the hill were able to keep their secret. And the king thought his flowers were just as good as theirs; but they really were not. The turtle is still in the lake: but no one, except Teteena, has ever seen him close to; for when she goes to cross over the rainbow, she aways goes alone.

TAL FORGOT everything while he was listening to the story. When it was done, he looked up and said, "Is that really true? The turtle must have been awfully big."

"It was," said Noom-Zor-Noom.

"Big enough to carry me on his back?" asked Tal.

"You . . . and me too," said Noom-Zor-Noom. "Look! There's the boat."

Tal looked around and saw that a boat had come to shore right next to the flat rock. It was not like any boat that he had ever seen in the harbor at Martoona: for it had no masts, and it had no sails. And instead of being shaped like most boats, it was round and looked exactly like a big silver bowl.

"Let's you and I go right over," said Tal, taking the old man by the hand.

"First I must put the block back on Millitinkle's back," said Noom-Zor-Noom. He did as he said; then

he went off down the beach with Tal, leaving the donkey
to follow behind.

After they had gone a good distance, and Tal had
looked back to make sure that Millitinkle could not hear
him, he said, "I'm awfully hot with this coat on. Will
it be all right if I take it off?"

"Why not?" asked Noom-Zor-Noom.

"I'm afraid of what Millitinkle might think," said Tal.
"I'm more like her if I have this fur on."

"She won't care," said Noom-Zor-Noom, smiling to
himself. "She's forgotten about that already."

So Tal took off his coat and carried it on his arm; and
he and the old man hurried across the beach to the rock.
When they got there, Tal saw that the boat was all made
of silver, and that there was a silver gangplank leading
up to it from the shore. Up this they walked. As soon
as Millitinkle, who was last, stepped on board, the gangplank disappeared: it could be seen no more.

The deck of the boat turned out to be silver too, and a
silver rail surrounded it. Equally spaced around the inside of the rail were seven silver lions' heads, each holding the handle of a silver basket in its mouth. Each
basket was filled with fruit: one with oranges, one with
pears, one with bananas, one with plums, one with
apples, one with peaches, and one with pomegranates.
In the middle of the deck was spread a big ermine rug,
and on it were three ermine pillows. That was all there
was on board, nothing else.

The prow of the boat stood out like a beak from a bowl, with three steps leading up into it. At the peak of the prow was a silver lyre, both arms of which were fashioned after the head and neck of a swan. On either side, under the curve of the swan's neck, passed six silver reins, making twelve in all. They fell on to the deck in loose coils, as if waiting for some one to pick them up.

Tal ran up in the prow and looked over the rail. In the water below he saw twelve silver dolphins with the silver reins in their mouths. While he stood there looking at them, Noom-Zor-Noom came and took hold of the reins. He shouted to the dolphins, and immediately they began to swim, pulling the boat behind them. Away they went through the waves, straight out to sea, on their way to Troom with the silver boat.

CHAPTER V

THE HOLE IN THE SEA AND THE STORY OF THE CLOUD

FOR THREE DAYS and three nights they sailed across the sea in the silver boat. Not once did the dolphins stop, but always they went on in the same direction. Noom-Zor-Noom stood in the prow all the time, holding the reins in his hands. He was quiet and solemn, and he looked as if his mind were filled with thoughts that worried him. He never spoke; he never ate; he only stood there, scanning the sea with his bright red eyes.

Tal watched him and thought to himself, "What's the matter with Noom-Zor-Noom? He's never acted like this before. I wonder if . . . Isn't it funny the way the wind blows his beard? I wonder if I'll be able to grow one like that some day? It would be fun to pull it. But I won't go near him: not unless he calls me. I guess he doesn't want to be bothered." Therefore Tal stayed where he was, for he knew it was the best thing to do.

As the days passed, the sea became calmer and calmer, until there were no waves at all. Then the breezes began to play music on the silver strings of the lyre, and the music made Tal drowsy. So he stretched out on the ermine rug and went to sleep. When he woke up, he ate his fill of fruit, then went to sleep again. And Millitinkle did the same.

On the fourth day, Noom-Zor-Noom looked back and said, "Tal, come here!"

Tal jumped up, half afraid that after such a long silence the old man was going to scold him about something. But what it might be, he could not think. He ran up into the prow and asked, "What do you want?"

"This afternoon," said the old man, "we shall reach the Hole in the Sea. I've been watching for it all along. If you see it before I do, let me know."

With these words that Noom-Zor-Noom spoke, Tal felt a great relief. He asked, "What do you mean by the Hole in the Sea? How can there be a hole in the sea?"

"There can," said Noom-Zor-Noom. "Right in the middle of the sea there is a great mountain. At the top of the mountain there is a hole just like the crater of a volcano. Down that hole we must go, for this sea that we are on now does not lead to Troom."

"Won't it be dangerous?" asked Tal.

"Of course it will," said Noom-Zor-Noom. "But I've been thinking about it, and I'm sure we can get down all right."

"What happens to us after we go down?" asked Tal.

"We'll come to another sea that lies under this one," said the old man. "And if we can cross that sea, we'll be somewhere near Troom."

"But I don't see how there can be another sea under this one," said Tal. "I thought there was solid ground under the water."

"There is under most seas," said Noom-Zor-Noom. "But this one is different."

"What's the difference?" asked Tal.

Just then Millitinkle sat up on her hind legs, flapped her ears, and said, "The difference is just this. Under most seas there is land, but under this one there is another sea. Now, if there are two seas, one over the other, and you want to get from the upper to the lower, how are you going to do it? The easiest way is to find a hole in the upper one that will take you down to the one underneath. What could be simpler?"

"Nothing," said Tal.

"Then you know what the Hole in the Sea is for," said Millitinkle, lying down again. "It leads from one sea to the other. And we have to go down it to get to Troom."

"Yes," said Tal. "I understand now."

When they had finished talking, Tal looked up and saw in the distance what seemed to be the top of a mountain. He pointed to it and asked, "Is that the mountain of water over there?"

"That's it," said Noom-Zor-Noom, pulling on the

reins and turning the dolphins in the direction he wished to go. "We'll soon be there now."

"But it looks like any other mountain," said Tal, a little disappointed. "Only it's all green and blue."

"It is like any other mountain," said the old man. "But it's made out of water instead of rocks and earth."

Before long they had sailed close to the foot of the mountain. And in another moment the dolphins began to swim up the mountainside, pulling the boat behind them. It was exactly like going up the side of a tremendous wave. Up and up they went, until they reached the top. And there, not far from where the boat stopped, Tal saw a big hole. He was not near enough to look far down it. But he could see that it was wide and black. And he heard a queer rumbling sound down below.

"The dolphins leave us here," said Noom-Zor-Noom. "They can go no further. We must go down the hole alone in the boat." With these words he cast the reins over the side of the boat. By this the dolphins knew that they were free to go where they pleased. And they swam away down the side of the mountain and disappeared.

"There's something in that hole!" said Tal. "I hear a rumbling."

"You hear waves being made," said the old man. "All the waves are made down there. A great part of the hole is full of waves. Whenever there are not enough on the ocean, they bubble out of this hole, roll down the mountainside, and go off across the sea. Every kind of wave comes from here, big and small alike. It's where they're all made."

"But," asked Tal, "how can we go down, if it is full of waves?"

"They only take up part of the hole," said Noom-Zor-Noom. "The rest is a passage that leads to the sea that's under this one."

"What would happen if waves started coming up, while we were going down?" asked Tal.

"We'd be wrecked," said Noom-Zor-Noom. "But we have to risk that."

All the time, while Tal and Noom-Zor-Noom were talking, the silver boat was drifting nearer and nearer to the Hole in the Sea. Before they quite reached it, Noom-Zor-Noom pulled aside the ermine rug and opened a trap door in the silver deck. Down through this they all three went; and they took the crystal block with them. After shutting the trap door, they found themselves in a round room that took up the entire inside of the boat. It was bare and empty and was lighted by seven windows. Noom-Zor-Noom made Tal sit against the wall on one side, and he put Millitinkle on the other. Then he placed the crystal block in the middle of the room and sat down on it himself. He said to Tal, "Don't be afraid. No matter what happens, stay where you are!" Hardly had he spoken, when the boat gave a lunge and slipped over the side of the hole. Then it began to spin and whirl like a top. It went down and down and down. The farther down it went, the faster it spun, until Tal felt himself being flattened out like a pancake against the wall. He looked across the room, and there was Millitinkle all flattened out too: she looked like a rug. But Noom-Zor-Noom, who was sitting right in the middle, did not change at all. In this way they whirled down through the Hole in the Sea. At last the boat stopped spinning so fast, and slowly Tal began to puff up to his own natural shape again. And by the time the boat stopped spinning altogether, he and Millitinkle were the same as they had been before.

"Now," said the old man, "look out of the window, and you'll see where we are." So Tal looked out, and he saw that the boat was floating on a bright red sea. And not far ahead, in the same direction as they were drifting, was a black island. "What's that island?" asked Tal. "Is that where we are going?"

"Yes," said Noom-Zor-Noom. "If we can drift that far."

They all went up on deck and found that everything had fallen out of the boat: the rug and the pillows were gone; so were the baskets of fruit. Noom-Zor-Noom sighed and said, "We have no dolphins to pull us along. We are just drifting. If we reach that island, all will be well. There we shall leave our boat and continue to Troom in something else."

"We can't go in anything but a boat," said Tal. "How can we?"

"Maybe not," said the old man. "We'll see when we get there."

After a while they reached the island, and the boat came to shore on a beach of black sand. There they landed. They took the crystal block ashore and set it on the beach. That night they slept by the sea. And before Tal went to sleep, Noom-Zor-Noom read him this story —the story of

THE CLOUD

THERE was a boy named Shandi. He was the son of a poor fisherman. All his life he had known how to fish, because his father always took him along wherever he went. In this way Shandi learned many things. He could tie on his own hooks; he could put on his own bait; and he could cast almost as far as his father could. Because he became such a good fisherman, his father often used to let him go fishing alone. When he did this, Shandi used to go to a big pool that was at the bottom of a very high cliff. He would sit at the top of the cliff and drop his line down into the pool, where there were a great many fish of all sizes and every kind. He almost always caught something, now one fish, now five, and sometimes even as many as ten.

One day Shandi was fishing from the top of the cliff. He had been fishing for a long time, when all of a sudden a big fish took hold of the bait. It was much bigger than any fish he had ever caught before; and it pulled so hard that it was all Shandi could do to hold on to the pole. He dug his heels into the ground and pulled with all his might, but he was not strong enough to get the fish out of the water. The harder he pulled, the more the pole bent, until it was bent almost double. The fish swam around, splashed, and wiggled its tail. In this way it managed to stay in the pool, for it did not want to come out. The harder *it* pulled, the harder Shandi pulled. And there they stayed just as if they were having a tug of war.

They might have stayed that way all day, had not something happened: the fish got the hook out of its mouth. This happened so quickly that Shandi fell over backwards into the bushes. The pole straightened out with a snap, and the line went flying into the sky. The hook caught in the side of a little white cloud, and there it stayed: it did not come down. When Shandi saw that he had caught a cloud instead of a fish, he began at once to pull in the line. As he did, the cloud circled round and round and came nearer and nearer to the earth. At last it came all the way down. And just as it touched the ground, a little door opened and out popped a funny little fat man. He was all blue in color, he had a long silver beard, and his body looked like a small balloon. He took one look at Shandi and said, "I am Faffa-Fuff the cloudman. I have always wanted to come to earth.

You have made this possible. Tell me what you wish, and I will grant it."

"I'd like to go up in your cloud with you," said Shandi.

"That's easy," said Faffa-Fuff. He stepped back inside the cloud; and when he came out, he had a little round gold box in his hand. This box had in it twelve pieces of what looked like candy; only each piece had a yellow half and a blue half. After Faffa-Fuff had broken all twelve pieces in half, he put the blue ones back in the box and hid the box under the root of a tree, where Shandi could find it. Then he said, "You are not very big. Twelve should be enough for you. Take two now!" He gave the boy two pieces, and he ate them. "Now jump," said the cloudman. Shandi jumped; but he only went a little way off the ground and then fell down with a thump.

"Two more," said Faffa-Fuff.

Shandi ate them. Then he jumped again. And this time he went further up than he had before, and he did not fall down quite so hard.

So the boy went on eating two yellow candies at a time. And each time after he ate two, he jumped. He kept jumping higher and higher and coming down with less and less force. After he had eaten all twelve candies, Faffa-Fuff said to him, "Now give a big jump." With these words, the cloudman jumped too; and they both went up and came down as if they did not weigh anything at all. Faffa-Fuff said, "Now you don't weigh any more than I do. When we come back from riding in the cloud, you must quickly eat all the blue candies. Then you will be yourself again and will be able to walk on the ground. The way you are now, the least wind that blew would carry you away."

"I like to be this way," said Shandi. "It would be fun to be blown by the wind."

"But you might get blown away and never come back," said the cloudman. "You wouldn't like that, would you?"

"No," said Shandi.

"Come," said Faffa-Fuff. "Take the hook out of the cloud; we'll go up."

Shandi took the hook out. Then he and the cloudman went into the cloud and shut the door behind them. As soon as the door was shut, the cloud began to move and drifted slowly up into the sky.

Inside of the cloud was a large square room. But instead of having solid walls like most rooms, its walls were made of thousands and thousands of silver threads that looked more like spiders' webs than anything else. They were soft and silky, and Shandi could look right through them down to the earth below. All the while the sunlight was playing in them, making them sparkle and glisten in a most marvelous way.

"See that big cloud up there?" said Faffa-Fuff. "We are going to go inside it and change its color."

Shandi looked out; and not very far away was a cloud

F

as big as any he had ever seen before. It was all fluffy and white, and it stretched away into the sky for miles and miles and miles.

"We'll have to go around behind it. That's the only way we can get in," said the cloudman. No sooner had he spoken, than the little cloud began to move through the sky very fast. It seemed to obey every wish Faffa-Fuff had, whether he spoke it or not. In a few minutes they had sailed behind the big cloud, and the next thing Shandi knew they flew right into the middle of all the fluff. It was like going into a very thick fog. Only, strangely enough, Shandi had the power of seeing through it all. He could see the sun, he could see the earth, and he could see many other clouds far beyond.

Once inside the big cloud, the little cloud came to a stop: it moved no more. Faffa-Fuff opened a closet in the wall and took out a golden bowl. Then he took out a golden tripod and set the bowl on it. He put both of them in the middle of the floor, passed his hand over the bowl, and it filled with water.

"What are you going to do?" asked Shandi.

"Change the color of the cloud," said Faffa-Fuff. "That's my job. Every night I color the clouds and arrange the sunset."

"I thought you had to paint things to change their color," said Shandi.

"Most people do," said Faffa-Fuff. "But I have a better way. Watch what I do, and you'll see."

After he spoke these words, the cloudman blew on the floor between the legs of the tripod, and a fire blazed up. Then he took out a wand and held it up for Shandi to see. It was not black like most wands, but it was bright orange, brighter than any orange Shandi had ever seen. The little man dipped the tip of the wand in the water, and the water became orange too. Before long the water began to boil. And when it boiled it gave off an orange steam that colored everything it touched. By the time all the water had boiled away, not only were the little cloud and big cloud all orange, but both Shandi and Faffa-Fuff were that color too.

"What do you think of that?" asked the cloudman.

"It's awfully pretty," said Shandi. "But I don't want to be orange all my life."

"Don't worry," said Faffa-Fuff, bursting into a loud laugh. "I can change you back any time you want."

After that they left the big cloud and hurried off to many, many other clouds. In every one they did the same thing; only they did not always use the same color, for Faffa-Fuff had many wands of different colors. Some clouds he made gray, some silver, some red, some yellow, some golden, and some pink. And every time he did it, Shandi himself changed color. After they were all through, Faffa-Fuff changed Shandi back to his own color, and he left the little cloud golden.

"Now," said the cloudman, "the sunset is all arranged. What would you like to do?"

"Can we go and see the sun?" asked Shandi.

"Not quite yet," said the cloudman. "It's too hot right now. Wait until it gets down a little lower."

So for a while they floated through the sky in their golden cloud. Shandi had such a good time that he thought he would like to stay up there forever. At last the sun went down far enough so that just a golden tip was peeping over the horizon. Then Faffa-Fuff thought it would be safe to go near. So they sailed straight into the sun, and the light got so bright that Shandi had to close his eyes. He got hotter and hotter and hotter. Although Faffa-Fuff kept telling him not to be afraid, he could not help thinking that they might run into the sun and be burned up. Finally it got so hot that even Faffa-Fuff could stand it no longer. So they turned back and went away. When Shandi opened his eyes, he saw lying on the floor of the cloud a pile of little golden drops.

"What are those?" he asked, pointing to them.

"They dropped off the sun," said Faffa-Fuff. "That shows how close we were. You can have them, if you want."

Shandi picked them all up and put them in his pockets.

"Are they pure gold?" he asked.

"Yes," said Faffa-Fuff. "There's enough gold in them to make you very rich!"

"I'll take them back to my mother," said Shandi. "She is very poor and needs some money."

"But don't tell her where you got them," said Faffa-Fuff.

"What shall I say?" asked Shandi, for he did not know how he could explain to his mother.

"Tell her the cloudman gave them to you," said Faffa-Fuff. "She'll understand."

Already the sky was getting dark and the color was fading out of the clouds. Faffa-Fuff knew that if Shandi was to get home before night, he would have to take him down soon. So he turned to him and said, "You alone can get me down. Lie on the floor and wish and wish and wish that you were back home."

This was not an easy thing for Shandi to do, for he really did not want to go back home. However, he lay down on the floor and wished as hard as he could. But the cloud showed no signs of going down.

"You're not really wishing," said Faffa-Fuff. "That's why the cloud won't go down."

Then Shandi began to think what fun it would be to surprise his mother with the gold. And soon the cloud began to drop little by little, until it came to earth on exactly the same spot where Shandi had been fishing. Faffa-Fuff opened the door and let the boy out. Then he said, "Go right over and eat the blue candies, or you'll be blown away."

"I don't want to," said Shandi. "I want to stay as I am."

"You can't," said Faffa-Fuff. "You'll be blown away.

If you want to get home at all, you'll have to eat at least one. I'll wait here while you do it."

Shandi went over to the root where the golden box was hidden and ate one of the candies. It tasted so good, that he had to eat another. And he went right on eating them, until all twelve were gone. Then he weighed just as much as he had weighed before, and he could hardly jump up in the air at all. He came back to Faffa-Fuff and said, "They were so good that I ate them all."

"That's just what I thought you'd do," said the cloud-man. "Now I want you to do me a favor."

"What is it?" asked Shandi.

"I have never spent a night on earth," said Faffa-Fuff. "I can't change my weight; so I can't walk on the ground. But if you hold on to me, you can take me home with you. We can tie the cloud here with a piece of your fishing line. Will you take me?"

"Of course I'll take you," said Shandi. "But I have a better idea. I'll put my hook in the seat of your trousers; then you can't blow away from me."

So they agreed to that. They tied the cloud to a tree. Then Shandi put his fishing hook in the seat of Faffa-Fuff's trousers and held on tight to the line. In this way they started off for Shandi's house. Every time a puff of wind blew the cloudman into the air, the boy pulled him back to earth again. When they got to the boy's house, Shandi went in alone with one end of the line in his hands and told his mother all that had happened to him.

Then he showed her the gold; and she asked, "Where did you get that?"

"The cloudman gave it to me," he said.

"Why didn't you bring him home with you?" asked his mother.

"I did," said Shandi. He pulled on the line and Faffa-

Fuff came bounding into the house. "Here he is, Mother. He's come to spend the night."

When Shandi's mother saw the cloudman, she was pleased. She took the hook out of his trousers and made him sit down. Then she cooked him such a supper as she had never cooked before. And Faffa-Fuff ate it and spent that night at Shandi's house.

The next morning they tried to persuade the cloudman to stay longer. But he would not. He said, "I must be going. The clouds will become very dull if I don't color them." So Shandi took him back to his cloud, and he went away up into the sky.

All the gold made Shandi's mother and father very rich. But this did not change Shandi's life at all. He kept right on fishing from the top of the cliff. But he never caught the big fish, nor did he ever catch another cloud.

CHAPTER VI

THE BLACK ISLAND AND THE STORY OF THE GREEN HORSE

THIS BLACK ISLAND that they landed on was the sleeping place of the whales. Whenever a whale in any part of the sea grew tired and wanted to sleep, he always came to this island and crawled up on the beach and went to sleep. There he stayed as long as he wished, for nothing ever happened to wake him up. Only sleepy whales came to the island. And by the time they got there, they were too tired to bother any of the other whales that were already asleep. So the island was a quiet, peaceful place, except, perhaps, when a big whale suddenly began to snore.

The first thing the next morning, as soon as Tal woke up, Noom-Zor-Noom took him to the other side of the island and showed him the beach where all the whales slept. There he saw rows and rows of whales all stretched out on the warm, black sand; and all of them were fast asleep. At first the sight terrified him, for he had never seen anything like it before. But Noom-Zor-Noom told him that there was nothing more harmless than a whale. Then Tal went a little nearer, looked at them carefully, and asked, "How many do you think there are?"

"About a thousand," said Noom-Zor-Noom. "But even if there were a million, they'll do us no good, unless we can find one big enough."

"Big enough for what?" asked Tal.

"I knew you'd ask that," said the old man. "I mean big enough to carry us all. We have to leave the silver boat here. It will be no use to us on this red sea. So, unless we wish to stay here forever, we must get one of these whales to take us off."

"How shall we do that?" asked Tal. "Ride on his back?"

"Not at all," said the old man. "Who ever heard of riding on a whale's back? There's only one place where a whale can carry you: that's in his stomach."

Tal's big, blue eyes opened wide, and he looked up at Noom-Zor-Noom in surprise. "You mean that you and Millitinkle and I can all get into one whale's stomach?"

"Yes," said Noom-Zor-Noom. "And the crystal block too."

"How are we going to get in?" asked Tal. "We'll have to be swallowed, won't we? Then all kinds of funny things will happen to us. I don't think I'd like that at all."

"Don't worry," said the old man, seeing that Tal was alarmed. "We'll just find a big whale, make him open his mouth, and we'll walk in. It's very easy."

"Everything is easy for you," said Tal. "But I don't want to go into a whale's stomach."

"Why not?" asked Noom-Zor-Noom. "You're not afraid, are you?"

"Kind of," said Tal. "It would be dark and awful inside. I know I wouldn't like it." And to himself he half-way wished that the old man would say something about going home. So many strange things had happened already, that Tal once or twice had thought that Noom-Zor-Noom might be taking him to a place from which he would never come back. Of course, it was not a very big thought, but it was just there in the back of his mind. And now it bothered him. He said, "It would be more comfortable for the whale if just you and Milli-tinkle went. You leave me here."

"That would be a nice thing to do," said the old man. "I've got to have you with me. Unless you hear my stories and pick out the one you like best, I'll be thrown into prison. You wouldn't want that to happen, would you?"

"No," said Tal. "I don't want anything to happen to you. But you're so mysterious and different from any one else, that sometimes I get scared. That's all."

"You needn't," said Noom-Zor-Noom. "If you want me to, I can change you into a person just like myself."

"I don't want you to," said Tal. "I'd rather be as I am. It's fun for us to be different."

"That's what I thought," said the old man. "But you

mustn't be afraid. Nothing is going to happen to you."

"I know it isn't," said Tal. "I'll go anywhere with you. I'm really not afraid."

"Of course you're not," said Noom-Zor-Noom. "Come along, we must look for a whale."

So Tal and Noom-Zor-Noom walked up and down the beach between the rows of sleeping whales. At last they came upon a huge whale, so large that at first they mistook him for two. When they saw that he was only one, the old man said, "Here's the whale for us."

"But his mouth isn't open," said Tal. "How can we get in?"

"That's all right," said Noom-Zor-Noom. "I'll get it open."

Then the old man and the boy went back to where they had left Millitinkle and the crystal block. They picked up all their belongings and carried them over to where the big whale lay asleep. Noom-Zor-Noom opened the end of the crystal block and took out the silver wand and the golden ball. Then, with a great deal of care, he touched the whale right on the end of the nose with the wand. He touched it once . . . twice . . . three times. And at the third touch, the whale's mouth opened slowly, just as if it were going to yawn. Wider and wider it opened, until Tal found himself standing in front of what looked like a big cave. He turned to Noom-Zor-Noom and asked, "Do we have to go down there?"

"Yes," said the old man.

"You've used the wand," said Tal. "But what are you going to do with the golden ball?"

"I'll show you in a minute," said Noom-Zor-Noom. "First we'll have to wait here until the whale gets used to sleeping with his mouth open. That won't take long. I don't think he even knows it is open. But it wouldn't be wise to go in too soon. He might close his jaws and crush us."

So they sat down where they were. And while they waited for the whale to go sound asleep, Noom-Zor-Noom read Tal the story of

THE GREEN HORSE

THERE was a horse, all green. He belonged to a man who made his living by working in the fields. The horse was so strong and could do so much work, that the man made a fair amount of money. He lived well and took good care of his horse.

The years went by, and the man grew old. But the

horse stayed just the same as he always had been. Why this was, no one knew. But every year on a certain day the horse disappeared and was gone for a month. The man never said a word and never scolded the horse for running away. For he had a feeling that if the horse did not do this, the animal would grow old. So whenever the horse came back, the old man welcomed him and gave him a lot of hay.

One day this man was plowing with his green horse. As he followed the plow, he stumbled on a rock, fell, and hurt himself so badly that he could not walk. No matter what the doctors did, nothing would cure him. He had to stay in the house all the time and could only move about with a great deal of pain. He thought, "The end has come for me. I have spent all my money on doctors, and they have done me no good. There is not enough left to keep both me and my horse alive. What can I do?" But there was nothing he could do, except to get poorer and poorer and poorer. And he and the horse lived on with hardly enough food to keep them alive.

Finally something had to be done: they could not go on starving forever. The man said to himself, "Two things I must do: I must find a good home for my horse, and I must make myself enough money to live on for the rest of my life. It is not right that the horse should suffer on my account. It would be good if I could sell him to some one who would promise to treat him well. The money I'd get would give me what I need to live on.

That seems to be the only way out of my trouble: there is no other." Thus he thought. But he hated to do it, for he loved the horse more than anything else in the world. Just the same, he made up his mind to sell him: but only to such a person as would treat the horse kindly, and only for such a price as so wonderful an animal should bring. Although he knew that this was the most sensible course to take, he hoped deep in his heart that no one would buy the green horse.

When the people heard that the green horse was to be sold, many buyers came. Among these were three brothers. They came to the man and said, "We want your horse. Sell him to us, and we'll give you three times as much money as any one else."

The man did not want to sell his horse to these three brothers, because no one liked them. But he had to have the money. He waited as long as he could to see if some one else would not offer the same price. But no one did. So he said to the three brothers, "I'll sell you my green horse, but only on condition that you treat him well. If you don't promise me this, you can't have him."

The brothers answered him with kind words. They pretended that they loved animals with all their hearts. They said, "You sell us your horse, and we will treat him just as well as you do. We will work him only a little, just enough for his own good. And we will give him all he wants to eat. You need not worry: he will be well taken care of."

"There's one thing more," said the man. "Every year he goes away for a month. If you buy him, you must be willing to let him go." And he told them on just what day the horse would disappear.

The brothers said, "We shan't mind if he goes for six months. He can do what he pleases with us. It's only that we feel sorry for you and want to give the horse a good home. That's why we wish to buy him."

The old man believed their kind words. He told them they could have the horse. He took their money; and the three brothers went off, leading the green horse behind them.

No sooner had they got the horse, than they began to think how hard they could work him. The oldest one said, "He is strong. We can work him day and night. We shall be able to plow more land than any one else. Soon we will become very rich, twice as rich as we are now."

With this in mind they took the horse home and tied him up in their barn. But they did not leave him there long. They hitched him to a plow, and day after day they worked the poor animal nearly to death. They gave him very little to eat, and often they let him go all day long without any water to drink. For they were not thinking of the horse, but only of the money they could make out of him. This was just greed on their part, for they had all the money they needed. But they did make a great deal more, many times as much as they had paid for the horse. And all the while the green horse grew thinner and thinner, but he never lost his strength.

At last the day came near for the horse to go away. The youngest brother said, "I wonder where this green horse goes? It would be good if we could find out. Then we might do the same and always stay young and strong. I think I'll ride on his back and find out where he goes." When the youngest brother spoke these words, at once the other two wished to go. So they argued and talked, until they finally agreed that all three of them would go. And it was all they could do to wait for the day to come on which the horse would disappear.

Early in the morning of that day, the three brothers went and fed the horse well. They patted him and said good-bye, as if they did not expect to see him for a month. Then they went out of the barn and left the door open, so the horse could get away. But instead of going back to the house, they waited round the corner, with the intention of jumping on the animal when he came out. All day long they waited, but nothing happened. They began to think they had been fooled, and that the horse had left the barn by some other way. Just as it was getting dark, they heard the horse move. Slowly he walked to the barn door, stuck his head out, and looked around. Seeing nothing, he walked out. But before he could get away, the three brothers, one after the other, jumped on his back and held on with all their strength. The horse paid no attention to them.

G

He trotted down the road, through the village, and off towards the mountains.

Night came, still the horse went on. He left the road and went through a rocky, wild country, where there were no houses and no men. He stretched his neck out and started to run. As he ran, green flames shot out of his nostrils; and his hoofs clanked on the rocks, striking green sparks that flew in every direction. The three brothers were frightened; they did not know where they were going. But all they could do was hold on as tightly as possible and gasp for breath. Soon the horse went around the side of a mountain and came to the edge of a steep cliff. As far down as the men could see there was nothing but darkness. Along the edge the horse ran at a terrific speed. Then he made a sudden turn and jumped wildly into space. The youngest brother, who was sitting behind, slipped off and fell. And before the horse had gone very far through the air, he had got rid of all three brothers. At last he came down on the top of a cliff on the other side and ran off to no-one-knows-where.

The youngest brother, the one who fell off first, dropped and dropped and dropped, until he landed on the top of a big haystack. He bounced up and down many times, and finally rolled off on to the ground with a jar. He picked himself up and looked around. He could see nothing. So he spent that night sleeping by the haystack, and in the morning he set out to find his way home. He walked a long way without seeing a house or a man. At last he came to the edge of some woods. He was about to go through them, when he heard a voice cry, "Help, help, help!" He turned aside in the direction where the voice came from, and there he found one of his brothers lying in a clump of brambles. The youngest brother said, "What are you doing here? I thought you were going to stay on the horse."

The second brother said, "I too fell off, I landed in these brambles. All night long I have been here in pain. It is a wonder I wasn't killed, I fell so far. Come, help me out; and we'll go home."

So the youngest one helped his brother out. And together they walked through the woods. All that day and all the next they walked without seeing any one. They had nothing to eat and nothing to drink; and the sun nearly burned them up with its heat. They got so thirsty that they could go no further. So they looked everywhere for a well, and finally they found one. The second brother looked down the well to see where the water was; and a voice from the bottom said, "Help me out of here, I am drowning." So he made a rope out of vines and dropped it down the well. They both took hold to pull it up, and whom should they pull out but their own brother. He said, "You have saved me, I was just about to drown." And he told them how he had fallen off the green horse and dropped into the well. Then they were all glad to be together again. They sat down and talked and wondered how they could find their way home.

After that they wandered for three months, until they came to a house. There a man told them how to get home. They followed one road after another, and as they went along they begged for food and drink. But so thin were they and so horrible looking, that the people were afraid to let them in their houses. Now some one would throw them a crust of bread or a piece of meat, that was all. In this way they got enough to keep them alive. They traveled on and on, and at last they reached home.

When the people in the village saw the three brothers, they laughed at them and said, "It serves you right. You weren't content to own the green horse. You treated him badly and worked him hard. You even thought you could go away with him and find out his secret." And no one would have anything to do with them. They went home and looked in their barn: the horse was not there. Then they were so ashamed, that they stayed only long enough to pack up their belongings. And in the night they sneaked out of the village and were never seen again.

The green horse, after having thrown the brothers off his back, stayed away a month, as was his custom. Then he came back. But he did not go near the barn of the men he had been sold to. He went straight to the house of the old man. He trotted up to the window, stuck his head in, and neighed loudly, so loudly that the old man, who was in the room, jumped with fright. When he turned around and saw his horse, he was glad. He thought, "I don't care how poor it makes me; I am going to buy my green horse back. He doesn't like those men. He wants to stay with me." With a great effort he limped over and stroked the horse's nose. Then he saw that the horse was holding something in his mouth. It looked like a small cherry and had a long stem. The animal kept holding it out, as if he wished the old man to take it. So the old man took it and ate it. And while he chewed, the horse neighed and looked very pleased. Then something wonderful happened. Suddenly the old man found that he could walk again. And at the end of a week he had just as much strength as he had before he was hurt. For the fruit was the same as what the horse ate when he went away for a month. So the man was able to keep the green horse. Again they worked in the fields together and plowed much land. And, as the three brothers never came back, the old man did not have to pay them their money. He and his horse worked hard, lived well, and were happy. And to this day no one has been able to find where the green horse went to get the fruit that kept him young.

"WHAT do you think of that?" asked Noom-Zor-Noom, after he had finished the story.

"I like it," said Tal. "But not as well as the one about Shandi. That was the best."

"That's what I want you to tell me," said the old man. "Say just what you think. Don't be afraid of hurting my feelings."

"I won't," said Tal. "But the whale must be asleep now. Can't we go inside him?"

Then they made ready to go down the whale's throat. The crystal block was put on Millitinkle's back, and she went first. She stepped on to the whale's lower jaw and walked carefully down his throat. After the donkey had disappeared from sight, Tal went in. He had not gone far before he found himself in a damp, dark tunnel, down which he felt his way as best he could. There was nothing to hold on to, and more than once he slipped and fell. But he managed to get down all right, even though it was so dark that he could not see his hand before his face. When he came to the end of the tunnel, it seemed to broaden into a big, black room: that was all Tal could make out. He said to himself, "This must be the whale's stomach. I don't know what else it can be." While he was groping around to try to find out where he was, he ran plumb into Millitinkle, who had been standing close to him all the time. He spoke to her and asked, "Is this the whale's stomach? Or do I have to go farther?"

Millitinkle flapped her ears; the little bells tinkled; and she said, "This is his stomach. You must stand still and not move. We don't want to wake him up before Noom-Zor-Noom comes. I don't think the whale will like the feeling of us in his stomach."

"I shouldn't think he would," said Tal. "I know *I* wouldn't."

"Then stand where you are and don't move," said the donkey.

The two of them stood close together without moving. Tal hardly dared to breathe, he was so afraid of waking the whale up. All the time they could hear Noom-Zor-Noom feeling his way down the throat. Finally he joined them. In the next moment he led Millitinkle a little way off and whispered to her, "Kick with all your strength."

Millitinkle did as she was told. She kicked her hind legs out with all her might, and they struck hard against the side of the whale's stomach.

"Once more," said Noom-Zor-Noom. "Do it harder, if you can."

Millitinkle kicked again. Then they heard the whale's mouth close with a snap; and everything began to move this way and that. There was a big wiggle and a big splash, and the whale slid into the sea and swam away.

CHAPTER VII

THE INSIDE OF THE WHALE AND THE STORY OF MILLITINKLE

ALTHOUGH Tal did not know it, Noom-Zor-Noom had carried the golden ball in his hand when he came down the whale's throat. And now, after it had been in the dark for some time, the ball began to glow. At first it glowed faintly and gave off only a poor light, about as much as comes from a big fire-fly. But it kept getting brighter and brighter, until soon it lit up the whole inside of the whale's stomach with a brilliant white light.

It was a long, low room with a vaulted ceiling. The ceiling was bright red, and so were the walls and floor. And when the light shone on them, they all sparkled, as if they were full of dancing flames and fire. It gave Tal the feeling of being inside a big ruby, the center of which had been hollowed out. From the ceiling, at the far end of the room, hung three hammocks; one woven of strings of sapphires, one of strings of diamonds, and one of strings of emeralds. On the floor under each of these stood a chest, studded with precious stones to match the hammock above it. That was all there was in the room.

When Tal saw how different everything was from what he expected, he said with surprise, "I didn't know a whale's stomach looked like this."

"Not all of them do," said Noom-Zor-Noom. "This one is very special; it belongs to the King of Whales. And the King of Whales has precious stones in his stomach, just as a king of men has them in the crown on his head."

"You mean he wears them there on purpose?" asked Tal.

"It's just his way of doing things," said the old man. "I suppose he does it on purpose."

"I'd rather have a crown," said Tal, still puzzled.

"Not if you were a whale," said Noom-Zor-Noom. "If a whale had a crown, it would come off when he swam. But as long as he wears his jewels in his stomach, he can't lose them."

"That's not what I was thinking of," said Tal. "People *can't* see your stomach, and they *can* see your head. It's much better to wear jewels where they can be seen."

"If you had a mouth as big as a whale's, people could look down and see your stomach," said the donkey, stepping up and putting her head over Tal's shoulder. "Then it would be nice to have one with precious stones in it. That's the answer to your question."

"You and your answers . . ." said Tal. "They make me . . ." He stopped short, not daring to finish his sentence.

"And you and your questions . . ." said Millitinkle. "You can ask more than any one I ever saw."

"Just the same," said Tal, "I'd rather have a crown. And, anyhow, I don't see why a whale wants to have his jewels made into hammocks."

"Because a 'hammocked stomach' means the same thing to a whale, as a 'crowned head' does to a man," said the donkey. "It's just a matter of taste, that's all."

"Whale's must have queer tastes, then," said Tal. "A crown is much better than a hammock."

"If a whale heard you say that, he'd think you were queer," said Millitinkle. "He wouldn't give up his hammocks for all the crowns in the world. It's just as well that he wouldn't, for the hammocks are nice to sleep in. Otherwise, we'd have to sleep on the floor."

"That's right," said Tal, "I hadn't thought of it that way."

"You should think of things in every way," said the donkey. "That's what I do."

For a good while after Millitinkle had finished these words, nothing more was said. Noom-Zor-Noom took the golden ball and set it down in the middle of the floor of the whale's stomach, where it burned brightly without giving off any heat. Tal went from one corner of the stomach to the other, looking carefully at everything he could find. He rubbed his hands over the jeweled chests, and he stood up on his tip-toes and swung one of the hammocks. He thought, "It'll be fun to sleep

in that. But I don't see how Millitinkle will ever get
up into hers. I hope she has to sleep on the floor. I
don't like the way she teases me." Then another thought
struck him, and he ran back to Noom-Zor-Noom and
asked, "What'll happen to us when the whale eats?"

"He won't eat," said Noom-Zor-Noom. "As long as
we live here and move about, he'll think his stomach is
full. So he won't be hungry."

Then the old man went on and told Tal how they
would have to spend two days and two nights in the
whale, before they would reach the other side of the sea.
The rest of that day they stayed where they were, and
Noom-Zor-Noom read the boy the story of

MILLITINKLE

MILLITINKLE used to be just like any other donkey.
She could not talk, she was not white, and she did not
have pink ears with little golden bells in the tops of
them. She worked hard for her master, carrying heavy
loads and making long journeys. And everything he
told her to do, Millitinkle did.

One time this man and his donkey were traveling up
in the mountains. For days and days they had been
making their way along narrow trails and over high
passes. At last they got so far up in the mountains that

soon they would be going down the other side. There they stopped at the foot of a cliff one night to sleep. The man put up his tent; and, as was his custom, he turned out Millitinkle to eat such grass as she could find. After doing this he rolled up in his blanket and went to sleep.

In the night it started to snow. But the man knew nothing about it, for he was asleep. It snowed and snowed. In the morning when the man woke up he started to go out of the tent, and a lot of snow fell in on him. He thought, "I am lost. There is no hope for me now. My donkey has probably been frozen to death. And I shall not be able to move from here until the snow melts. What a fool I was to leave the donkey outside." With much trouble he pushed his way out of the tent and climbed up on a snow drift. Everywhere he looked, in every direction, he could see nothing but snow. It was so deep that it was over his head. He called to Millitinkle, but she did not come. At last he gave up, went back into the tent, and made up his mind to wait. There was nothing else he could do. But his heart was sad, and he wept over the horrible fate that had befallen his donkey.

Now, when the snow began to fall, Millitinkle was a long way from her master. She had not found much to eat near by, so she had wandered down the mountainside in search of grass. She was busy grazing when the storm started. Before she realized what a bad storm it was, the snow was already so deep that she could hardly lift one leg after the other. Fright seized her. She turned this way and that way in hopes of being able to move. She brayed for help. But the wind carried her voice down the mountain instead of toward the tent. All the time the snow was falling fast and heavy. The more the donkey struggled, the deeper in she got. Finally the snow covered her over completely and she felt nice and warm. "This is not so bad," she thought. "I'll rest for a while and then burrow along. I might as well travel under the snow as on top. It's warm, and there's no wind down here." So she rested and slept a little; and afterwards she began to kick and paw and make a tunnel for herself underneath the snow.

In this way she traveled for some distance, always down hill, for that was the easiest way to go. Behind her she left a long tunnel where the snow had been pushed aside and trampled down. On she went and on. She was thinking that soon she would get out, when the snow in front of her fell away, and she found herself in a cave. The walls were all of ice, and a dim light shone through them. The floor was ice too, very smooth and very slippery. Millitinkle looked around at herself; she was pure white. The snow had changed her color, and no amount of licking or shaking would change it back. This rather pleased her. She said to herself, "Now I'll be different from all other donkeys. None of them are as white or as beautiful as I am. My master won't know me when he sees me again." Then she started off at a trot down through the cave, wondering what she was going to find.

This cave that Millitinkle came into was the entrance to the palace of the Snow Queen. There the Snow Queen lived alone with all the snow fairies whose task it was to make the snow-flakes and scatter them during a storm. But the donkey did not know this. She trotted on and on, until she found herself at the door of a big room. The room was lit up with a wonderful white light that seemed to come from nowhere. From the ceiling hung long icicles that glittered and sparkled with every color of the rainbow. The walls were of ice, but as clear and pure as crystal. In the middle of the room was a high throne made of blocks of ice. On this sat the Snow Queen. She was all dressed in white fur, and on her head she wore what seemed to be a diamond crown. But it was really made of beautifully cut pieces of ice. When she saw Millitinkle at the door, she said, "What are you doing here? Neither man nor animal has ever found his way here before. Come in and let me see you."

Millitinkle trotted in and made a low bow before the queen. The queen, seeing what a beautiful animal the donkey was, said, "In all my life I have never seen a white donkey. You must stay with me. I will keep you and feed you well. Will you stay?"

Millitinkle brayed and tried to make herself understood. But it seemed impossible to make the queen see

IN THE MIDDLE OF THE ROOM WAS A HIGH THRONE MADE OF BLOCKS OF
ICE. ON THIS SAT THE SNOW QUEEN.

what she was trying to say. At last the donkey stood there in silence and looked sadly at the floor.

The queen said, "I see what's the matter. You can't talk. Eat this, and you'll be able to." She handed Millitinkle a small cake all covered with white frost. As soon as the donkey swallowed it, she was able to speak just like a human being. Then Millitinkle told the queen all about what had happened. And when the queen heard the story, she said, "I will send you back to your master. But first you must stay a month with me. I am all alone here. And I want you for a friend. You stay a month: then you can go to your master."

Millitinkle asked, "Do you think he will be all right?"

"I know he will," said the queen.

So Millitinkle agreed to stay a month with the Snow Queen. She lived in the palace and had a happy life.

During this month the donkey learned many things she had not known before. The Snow Queen took her from room to room and showed her the snow fairies at work. They were little white people with silver wings. All day they worked hard making snow-flakes. They made them in many shapes and in many sizes. When they were made, they put them in little baskets that seemed to be woven out of frozen cobwebs. Then, when the queen wished to have a storm anywhere, the fairies flew forth with their baskets and scattered the flakes in the wind. All this Millitinkle saw. Also she met some ice fairies. These were almost without color; they could hardly be seen. But they had a wonderful power. For wherever they touched water with their feet, that water turned into ice. All of these people lived in the palace. They were very happy and very busy. And they all loved their queen.

In return Millitinkle told the queen many things about the world of men. To these the Snow Queen always listened with a great deal of interest, for she had never heard about them before. She came to like the donkey more and more. And she dreaded the day when the animal would have to leave.

One night, while they were eating together at a silver table, a fairy came in and said, "I have been to the man's tent. He is very lonely. All day long he sits and sighs for his donkey. In this way he cannot live much longer."

The queen said, "He won't have to wait many days more. His time is nearly up."

Millitinkle was sad and said, "It isn't fair that I should stay from him. Hadn't I better go?"

But the queen insisted that the donkey stay, saying, "If you go now, you will be sorry; for your master could not find you in the snow. When the month is up, I'll give you something to make you more beautiful than you are now. Then you can go, and your master will have no trouble finding you."

So Millitinkle said no more. But she wondered what the queen meant by her words.

Finally the month was up, and the time came for the donkey to leave. She said to the queen, "To-day I shall go away. You have been very kind to me and have treated me well. Now that I'm going, tell me what you are going to give me."

The queen said, "Come over here with me, where this red light from the icicle shines on the wall. You must do just as I tell you."

They walked over to the wall, and the queen made Millitinkle kneel down so that just her ears were shaded by the red light. Then she took a long, silvery icicle, and lightly touched the top of each ear. She said, "Now you have pink ears. Your master will be able to see you in the snow." But Millitinkle, who could not see her own ears, did not know whether the queen spoke the truth or not. "One thing more I want to do for you before you go," continued the queen. "I am going to give you a present to remember me by." And in the top of each of the donkey's ears she put a little golden bell. Then she said, "Now you can go. You are in every way the most beautiful donkey in the world. I wish you could stay with me forever."

Millitinkle thanked the queen for all she had done, saying, "I won't forget you. If I didn't have a master, I'd be glad to stay here. But I can't stay away from him any longer. Every time I think of you I'll do this." And the donkey shook her ears, and the bells went, "Tinkle, tinkle, tinkle."

So the queen and the donkey bade each other good-bye, and Millitinkle went off by the same way she had come. Out through the cave she trotted and down through the tunnel she had made in the snow. There, when she came to the end, she stopped to rest.

While she rested, the sun shone on the snow above her, and the snow melted. It melted enough so that her pink ears stuck out. And when she wagged them, the bells went "Tinkle, tinkle, tinkle." Her master who was sitting in the tent, heard this sound. He got up to look out, and he saw the pink ears. With a jump he was up and running through the snow. He thought, "What can those two pink things be? There's just a chance that they may be the ears of my donkey. Poor Millitinkle, she's frozen! That's why her ears are pink." He pushed his way on to where the donkey was. Just as he came near enough to see things clearly, Millitinkle stuck her head out of the snow and said, "Hello. Come help me!"

"Who is that?" said the man, for he could not believe that it was the donkey that spoke.

"Millitinkle," said the donkey. "Help me out, and I'll tell you how I learned to talk."

"Are you still alive?" asked the man, who was so surprised that he really did not know what he was saying.

"Of course I am," said Millitinkle. "But I'll freeze if you leave me here much longer."

Then the man dug the donkey out. And she told

him about the wonderful things that had happened to her: How she had learned to talk. How she got her pink ears. And why she had bells in them. And the man thought of nothing but how glad he was to have his donkey back. Together they made their way up to the tent. By the next day the snow had melted enough so that they could go on their journey. They were happy; they talked to each other; and they became the best of friends in the world.

AFTER the story had been told, Tal asked, "Is that true?"

"Yes," said Noom-Zor-Noom. "Every word of it."

"Then tell me how *you* happened to get Millitinkle," said Tal. "Why didn't the other man keep her?"

"Because there was no other man," said Noom-Zor-Noom. "All of that story really happened to Millitinkle and me. Didn't it, Millitinkle?"

The donkey smiled and nodded her head. "All that, and a good deal more," she said.

"Then I like it best of all," Tal said. "I always like stories when I know the people that they are about. It makes them much more real. It must have been wonderful at the Snow Queen's, wasn't it?" he added, hoping to make Millitinkle tell him about it. But she paid no attention to his question. She sat and gazed at the golden ball, as if enjoying thoughts that she had no idea of sharing with any one else.

"She won't tell you anything," said Noom-Zor-Noom. "She likes to keep it to herself."

"Then you tell me," said Tal. "I want to hear more."

"I can't," said the old man. "I've told you all that Millitinkle told me. The rest will never be known."

When it came time for supper, each of them opened one of the chests under the hammocks. In his, Tal found all his favorite things to eat, a big helping of each on a golden plate. And Noom-Zor-Noom and Millitinkle found the same. After they had had supper, they put the plates back in the chests and closed them up. Then it came time to go to bed. Noom-Zor-Noom lifted Tal up into the emerald hammock, and he himself climbed into the diamond one. Millitinkle stayed on the floor where she was. Tal pretended to go to sleep, but all the time he had one eye part way open, watching the donkey. He waited and waited to see what she was going to do. Finally, after a long time, she walked slowly toward her hammock. When she got near it, she suddenly gave a jump, turned half a somersault in the air, and landed on her back in the hammock. She did not move, but lay there just as she had landed and went to sleep with all four legs sticking straight up in the air. Then Tal fell asleep. And that night he swung in his emerald hammock and dreamed of all the wonderful things he had seen since leaving Martoona with Noom-Zor-Noom.

CHAPTER VIII

THE MELLIKANOO AND THE STORY OF THE MUSIC BOX

THE NEXT MORNING Tal got up and again opened his chest, and there he found breakfast all ready for him. When the boy had eaten his fill, Noom-Zor-Noom took him by the hand and led him back up the whale's throat. Near the animal's mouth, they turned off into a narrow passage. Following this for a short way they came to the end and found themselves in a little round room with two windows in it. This was the whale's head. The windows were like port-holes, and a red light was shining through them. They went up to one of the windows, and Noom-Zor-Noom said, "This is one of the whale's eyes. If you stand here, you can look out and see everything that the whale sees." Tal did as the old man told him. And when he looked out of the window, he saw all kinds of fish swimming in the red water. He saw sharks, octopi, sea-serpents, sword-fish, turtles, balloon-fish, and many other strange creatures. All these things Tal saw, and he could not make up his mind to go away. So he stood there the entire day looking out of the whale's eye.

In this way Tal traveled across the sea. The time

107

passed quickly, because he had so many things to watch. Before he knew it, the two days and nights were up, and he had not looked out of the whale's eyes half as much as he wanted to.

On the third day the whale came up for air, and Tal saw what seemed to be a forest growing out of the middle of the sea not far ahead. There was no land in sight, but only a lot of trees that rose from the surface of the water to a height of two hundred feet or more. Their branches, instead of being round, were square and so broad that a man could walk the length of one with no trouble at all. There were no leaves. But hanging from each branch were many, many round things that looked exactly like big magic lanterns. When Tal saw all this, he ran back down into the whale's stomach and said to Noom-Zor-Noom, "What's that ahead of us? It looks like a forest. But I've never seen one growing out of the middle of the sea. Come up and look at it!"

"I don't have to," said Noom-Zor-Noom. "I know what it is. It's the Land of Trees. We stop here: the whale takes us no further." With these words, he hurried and packed the crystal block on Millitinkle's back. "Pick up your bundle," he said to Tal. "If we don't get out in a hurry the whale will start to eat. This is where they feed, in among the roots of the trees that you saw. As soon as he bumps, follow me and Millitinkle as fast as you can." For a moment they stood still, waiting.

Then there was a terrific bump that almost knocked all three of them off their feet, and the whale came to a stop and floated to the surface. "Come on!" shouted the old man excitedly, and he started off up the whale's throat. After him went Millitinkle. And Tal followed behind, trying not to lose them in the darkness; for Noom-Zor-Noom had put the golden ball away, and there was no light.

Tal did the best he could to follow them, but he kept falling down and slipping back. Pretty soon he was so far behind that he could not even hear where the others were. He groped around and finally felt his way into a passage that he thought the others had taken. It led him round and round, until he came into a big, dark room. There he stopped and thought to himself, "This can't be the right way. I am lost." So he shouted and called at the top of his lungs. And every time he shouted, things seemed to shake and turn around, and he was thrown flat on his face. So he stopped shouting, lay down, and cried, "I'm lost! I'm lost! I knew something terrible like this would happen. Nobody will ever know what has become of me. I'll just stay here and die." And he wished that he had never been so foolish as to leave Martoona.

The donkey and the old man made their way out on to the top of the whale's head. They waited for Tal, but he did not come. As they stood there waiting, the whale shook his head and nearly threw them into the water. Then he shook it again and again and again. And he shook it so hard and so often, that Noom-Zor-Noom and Millitinkle had to save themselves by going back inside the passage by which they had come up. Even then they were badly bumped and bruised from being thrown about so roughly. And they might have been hurt a good deal more, had not the whale suddenly stopped.

"I know what's the trouble," said Noom-Zor-Noom, picking himself up.

"So do I," said Millitinkle, rubbing her forehead with her hoof. "Tal has lost his way and gone into the whale's ear."

"Just what I was going to say," answered the old man. "You stay here, and I'll go back after him."

"Do it as quietly as possible," begged Millitinkle. "I don't want to have another earthquake."

So the old man crept back to the whale's ear, and there he found Tal. He crawled up to him and whispered, "Don't say a word, follow me."

"I lost my way," sobbed Tal. "I didn't mean to . . ."

"Sh!" said the old man. "Not a word till we get out of here."

They crawled out and went up into the whale's head. From there they went into another passage, up a flight of circular stairs, and came to where the donkey was. Then the old man said, "No wonder the whale shook his head. He had an ear-ache. I found Tal right next to his ear drum."

"I didn't mean to do it," sobbed Tal. "I got lost."

"You nearly killed me," said Millitinkle, feeling very sorry for herself. "I'm all black and blue."

"I'm sorry. But I couldn't help it," said Tal.

"That doesn't make me feel any better," said the donkey. "Why didn't you follow us?"

"It wasn't his fault," said the old man, patting Tal on the shoulder. "Don't scold him. Come on, we've got to get out."

So they climbed out through a trap door on to the whale's head. And everything was peaceful and quiet, just as it should be.

After looking around a little, Noom-Zor-Noom pointed to the hole that the whale spouted out of and said to Tal, "You sit on that hole. The whale will blow you up into the tree."

"But I'll get all wet," said Tal. "I'll just go up and come down into the sea."

"No, you won't," said Noom-Zor-Noom. "You'll land on one of the branches. Don't be afraid."

Tal felt that he had caused enough trouble already. So he did as he was told; he sat down over the hole. The next minute the whale spouted, and Tal went shooting up into the air in a stream of water. He did not come down, but he landed gently on a big branch; and there he stayed. He shouted to Noom-Zor-Noom, "I'm all right. That was great fun. Are you coming up too?"

"I am in a minute," said the old man. "Millitinkle must go first."

Then Millitinkle did the same as Tal. And she and the crystal block were blown up on to the branch. After her came the old man. When they were all three together again, Tal said, "That whale has been good to us. I wish I hadn't given him that ear-ache. Wouldn't it be nice if I threw him something to eat?"

"I have a piece of whale food inside the crystal block," said the old man. "I'll get it for you, and you can throw it to him." He opened the crystal block and took out a huge piece of cheese and handed it to the boy. "Throw that down to him," he said. "Whales like cheese better than anything else." Tal took the piece of cheese and threw it down, saying, "Here you are, Mr. Whale. Thanks for the ride. I'm sorry I gave you an ear-ache. I didn't mean to." The whale opened his mouth and caught the cheese. Then he smiled, dived under the water, and swam away.

Tal, Noom-Zor-Noom, and Millitinkle sat on the end

of the branch until the sun dried them. Then they got
up and walked toward the tree. Near the trunk, right
where the branch grew out of the tree, they came to a
bird's nest, so big that all of them could fit inside it with
no trouble at all. They climbed into the nest and found
it full of golden feathers.

"What are these?" asked Tal, picking up a big golden
feather.

"They are the feathers of the Mellikanoo," said Noom-
Zor-Noom. "The Mellikanoo is the biggest bird in the
world, and he makes his home among these trees. Once
a day he flies away to drink water from the Zool river.
That's where he is now. If we can get him to carry us
to the Zool, we shall be all right. Because that river is
not far from Troom."

"How are we going to get him to take us?" asked
Tal.

"That's easy," said Noom-Zor-Noom. "The Mellikanoo is big, but his legs are small and weak. More
than that, his feet are very ticklish. If we can get hold
of the bird's feet and tickle them, he will grant us any
wish to make us stop."

"How are we going to do that?" asked Tal.

"I'll show you," said Noom-Zor-Noom.

Then the old man told them what he had in mind.
He and Tal set to work and wove all the golden feathers
into a big basket that exactly fitted the inside of the nest.
When this was done, they put the basket in the nest, and

all three of them sat down in the bottom. Noom-Zor-Noom said, "Here we must wait until the bird comes back. He will not come until after dark. If we are very quiet, he will settle on the nest without seeing us. Then I'll show you what to do."

All that afternoon they waited in the bottom of the basket. But they saw no sign of the Mellikanoo. Tal became restless: he wanted to see what was going to happen. He asked this question and that question; but the old man would tell him nothing. At last, in order to make the time pass more quickly, Noom-Zor-Noom uncovered the crystal block and read the story of

THE MUSIC BOX

THERE was a girl named Iantha. She lived in a palace with her mother. Her mother was so fond of her and so afraid that something might happen to her, that she never let Iantha go outside. Instead, she built her a big play room. And there Iantha grew up with all the toys that any child could want.

Now and then the mother gave a party for Iantha. She invited children from the village to come and play with her daughter. These children used to tell Iantha all about the outside world: How fresh and soft the grass was. How pretty the flowers were and how sweet they smelled. And how much fun it was to skip and run in the woods under the trees. All this made her very sad. And after the children had gone she used to sit in the window and cry quietly to herself.

One day her mother saw her and said, "What's the matter? Why are you crying?"

Iantha said, "I want to go outside and dance in the fields like the other children. I want to pick flowers and run in the woods."

Her mother said, "What could you do outside? You don't even know how to dance and sing. The other children would only laugh at you and make fun of you. Learn how to dance and sing; and then I'll let you go out."

Poor Iantha didn't know what to say. All her life she had tried to sing, but she couldn't. As for dancing, she had no wish to try it. But she felt that if once she got out in the fields, she would be able to do both just as easily as the other children. So she asked, "How can I learn in here? Let me go out just once, and you'll see me learn in no time at all."

"You'll not go out until you've learned," said her mother, for she knew that in this way she could keep Iantha to herself.

What could Iantha do? She cried and cried and begged her mother not to be so cruel. Finally her mother went away and left her. Still Iantha cried. And her tears fell on the floor and made a big pool. After a while she became so tired, that she went to sleep sitting on the window sill. Of course she slipped off and fell into the pool. This woke her up. She looked for the pool, it had gone. Her clothes had soaked all the tears up; and everything she had on had turned into gold. She had gold shoes, a gold dress, and a gold handkerchief. She knew that her mother would take these from her if she found them. So she took them all off, put on other things, and hid the golden clothes under the mattress.

On her next birthday, her mother gave her a beautiful gold music box all set with jewels. Iantha loved this more than any presents she had ever had. She used to play it and try to sing and dance to the tunes. In this way she learned a little bit about singing, just enough to scare her mother. So her mother forbade her to play it except for an hour in the morning. Iantha pretended she did not want to play it any more. Then, every night, after she was certain all the people in the palace were asleep, she would get up and start the music box. She would put on all her beautiful golden clothes and dance and sing as well as she could.

One night the moon was shining very brightly in the window. The music box had run down; and Iantha was feeling for the hole to put the key in, so she could wind it up. Just as she found it and was about to stick in the key, a soft little voice said, "Iantha, is that you?" Iantha looked to see where the voice came from, but she couldn't quite make out. Again she started to wind up the music box, and again the same little voice said, "Iantha, is that you?"

"It's me," said Iantha. "But where are you and what do you want?"

"I'm in the music box. Right here, feel with your finger." Iantha put her finger to the keyhole, and there she felt a tiny, tiny hand. "Wouldn't you like to come in?"

"Very much," said Iantha. "But I'm big and the box is small."

"You come in and we'll teach you how to dance and sing," said the little voice.

"But I'm too big," said Iantha.

"No, you're not. Give me your hand," said the voice.

At first Iantha was afraid. But when the little person in the box offered so kindly to teach her to sing and dance, she forgot all else. She took hold of the tiny hand and clutched it with all her strength. She felt herself shrinking, shrinking, shrinking. Then some one gave her a pull. And the next thing she knew she was through the keyhole and inside the music box.

She knew what the inside of a music box was supposed to look like. It had a big round barrel all covered with funny prickly things. But that wasn't what Iantha saw. She was standing in a wide, yellow field, and in every direction she saw trees and bushes. Everything smelled so nice and fresh, just like outdoors. "This is very nice," she thought, "to be outside like this. But who brought me here?" No sooner had she thought it, than a lot of children came skipping across the field in her direction. They were gay and happy and full of life.

"Iantha, Iantha!" they shouted. "Have you come to play with us?" When they saw the beautiful golden clothes she had on, they were all very much surprised. They said, "Look at her! look at her! She is all in gold. She must be our queen." Then they formed a circle and danced and sang about her.

"Where am I?" asked Iantha, for she couldn't believe what had happened to her. "Is this really the music box?"

"Of course it is," they shouted.

"But where is the great yellow round thing and all the prickly little black things?" she asked.

When they heard her say this, they laughed and shouted. "The field you're standing in is part of the yellow thing. The trees are the black things." Then they shrieked with joy and all ran up and took hold of her.

"Am I as small as all of you?" asked Iantha.

"Surely you are. That's how you got in. Now we're going to show you how to dance," they said, pulling at her clothes.

Iantha asked no more questions. She was too happy with all her new friends to think of anything but joining in the fun.

"Now you do just as we do," they said. They all joined hands, with Iantha in the middle, and then spread out across the field in a long line. "In a minute it will start," said the boy at her right. "When it does, you must dance and sing the same as we do." The next minute the field started to move. Then they all danced and sang, while the field moved by under their feet. They did not dare stay on the ground long, for fear of being carried down the steep slope behind them. The field passed by and a forest came. In all the trees birds were singing. After the forest went by, another field came. And so they danced through woods and fields, which passed by them, while they really jumped up and down in the same spot. It was so easy, that Iantha could do just as well as all the others. At last they stopped right in the center of a small field. And Iantha had time to catch her breath before they sang another tune. Then on they went again, dancing and singing, until Iantha had learned all the tunes that the music box played.

"I love it," she cried, her face flushed with excitement. "I could go on all night. It's such fun to be outside like this."

"Isn't it?" said the little boy. "But if you had to do it as much as we do, you might get tired."

"Oh, no, I wouldn't," she said. "I want to stay here forever with you. You are so nice to me."

In a minute all the children had gathered around her.

"Our Queen, our Queen," they shouted. "We are going to crown you queen." One of them rushed up and placed on her head a lovely crown all made of flowers. "Now dance!" they cried. And while they sang and -threw roses at her, Iantha danced. She had never been so happy in her life. It was such fun to be with these playful children out in the woods and fields. She could not bear the thought of ever having to leave them.

Her good time was over much too soon. The minute the first light of day shone in through the keyhole, the boy who had been more or less taking care of her said, "You must go now. Give me your hand, and I'll see that you get out all right." He led Iantha to the keyhole and held on to her hand while she crawled through. Then he squeezed her hand with all his might, and she grew bigger and bigger and bigger, until once more she was her own size. She hurried to take off her golden clothes and her crown of flowers. She put them back under the mattress and got into bed and went to sleep.

That morning, when her mother came to wake her up, Iantha said, "I have learned how to dance. Now you must let me go outside."

Her mother laughed at her and said, "You have been dreaming. How could you ever learn how to dance?"

"I have," said Iantha. "You go out of the room and don't come in till I call you. Then you'll see what I can do."

So her mother went out. Iantha got all dressed up in her beautiful clothes. She put on her crown, and started the music box playing. "All right," she said. "Come in." And when her mother came in, Iantha was dancing and singing more beautifully than could any of the other children in the village. Her mother couldn't take her eyes off her, she was so graceful and sang so sweetly. After she had sung all the tunes the music box played, she stopped and asked, "Now may I go out in the fields?"

"Where did you learn all this?" asked her mother, for she couldn't believe what her own eyes had seen.

"The music box taught me," said Iantha. "Would you like to see me do it again?"

She started again. While she danced, she went nearer and nearer the door. And before her mother knew what was happening, Iantha disappeared out into the hall. Down the hall she danced, and on down the stairs. Then she went right out at the front door. Not once did she stop to look back, but she skipped and ran across the fields just as fast as she could go. "This is even more fun than the music box," she thought to herself. "If I can only reach the woods before any one catches me, I'll be all right."

Finally she came to the edge of the woods. She ran in among the trees and sat down on a rock. She had not been sitting there long, before all the birds began to sing just as they had in the music box. And when Iantha looked up to listen, she saw all her little friends from the music box come running through the woods toward her. She said to them, "What are you doing

One of them said, "Your mother was very angry because you learned to dance. So she broke the music box and threw it away. We had to run to save ourselves."

"If she did that," said Iantha, "I'm not going back home."

So she stayed in the woods and lived with the little people from the music box. She was very happy with them, and they made her their queen again. She is still with them. And all day long she sings and dances through the woods and fields.

WHEN he was through reading the story, the old man opened the end of the crystal block, reached in, and pulled out a large coil of golden rope. He carefully laid it in the bottom of the basket, where he could easily reach it. But he did not say a word about what he was going to use it for.

Time passed; evening came. As soon as it was dark, all the round things that Tal had seen hanging from the branches began to fly about. As they flew, their bodies lit up with many different colors. When Tal saw them, he said, "What are those? They look too big to be fireflies."

"They are magic lantern flies," said Noom-Zor-Noom. "They only light up when the Mellikanoo is not here. When that bird comes, they go out. Because if they stayed lit, the Mellikanoo would catch them and eat them."

While Tal sat watching them fly above the nest, all

of a sudden they all went out. Then, from the distance, Tal heard a loud cry that sounded like, "Mellikanoo-kanoo-kanooooo." For a moment all was silent. Then again came the cry, "Mellikanoo-kanoo-kanoooooooo." Only this time it was much louder and sounded quite near. And when the bird cried for the third time, Noom-Zor-Noom whispered to Tal and Millitinkle, "Lie down flat in the bottom of the basket. Here comes the bird."

He had hardly spoken these words, when there was a flutter of wings and a great commotion in the trees just overhead. Then they heard the bird jump down on to the branch. The next minute two shining purple eyes looked over the edge of the nest. For a long time they looked, as if to make sure that everything was all right. Then the bird hopped and settled down on the nest with a loud squawk of satisfaction. That was all that Tal saw, for after that everything became pitch black.

CHAPTER IX

THE ZOOL RIVER AND THE STORY OF TRUMBILLOO THE MAGICIAN

AFTER the Mellikanoo had been on the nest for some time, he tucked his head under his wing and went to sleep. The sounder he slept, the louder he snored, until he was making a noise like thunder.

When Noom-Zor-Noom heard this, he was glad. For he then knew that he could do what he had in mind. Quietly he got up and took the coil of rope in hand. Carefully he fastened it to many places in the rim of the basket. Then he tied the ends to the Mellikanoo's legs, high up above the knees, where they could not come undone. All this he did without once disturbing the bird. And when it was done, he sat down in the bottom of the basket and whispered to Tal, "Stay right where you are, and don't move. What we are going to do now is more dangerous than anything we have done before. We may be able to do it, and we may not. But, whatever happens, you must stay absolutely quiet." With these words he took out his silver wand and began to tickle the bird between the toes.

The Mellikanoo woke up with a start. He laughed like a hyena and kicked his legs furiously. But no amount of kicking did him any good. His small, weak

legs only struck the sides of the basket, for they were not
long enough to reach down to the bottom. And all the
time Noom-Zor-Noom kept reaching up and tickling
the bird between the toes. Soon the Mellikanoo could
stand it no longer. He flapped his wings, rose from the
nest, and flew off into the sky, thinking that in this way
he could escape. But he was mistaken, for he carried
the golden basket with him. And Tal, Noom-Zor-
Noom, and Millitinkle were swept through the sky at
a terrific speed.

Now it was the custom of the Mellikanoo always to
fly straight up in the air before starting in any particular
direction. By doing this he got well out of sight before
any one could see where he was going. That night he
did the same. Up and up he went, shrieking and laughing for all he was worth. The higher he went, the
brighter the stars got, and the bigger the moon; so that
there was soon enough light for Tal to see the Mellikanoo quite clearly. His huge body was covered from

one end to the other with golden feathers. His tail was made of long, slender quills, each of which had a fan of feathers at the end. As he flapped his wings and flew, these fans opened and shut at different times, so that the whole tail seemed a mass of twinkling, golden lights. On account of the length of his neck, his head was far away. But not so far that Tal could not see a turned-up beak and two burning eyes that cast beams of purple light in whatever direction they looked. All this Tal saw, and he thought to himself, "What a wonderful bird! I wish I had one like him to take me everywhere I wanted to go. I could keep him in the house. And nobody else would have one like him."

When the Mellikanoo was so high up that even the earth was out of sight, he bent his neck, stuck his head back, and looked down into the basket. Then he said, "You have dared to do a thing that no one has ever done before. You have come to my nest and woven a basket out of my feathers. If you will stop tickling my feet, I will grant you what you wish."

Noom-Zor-Noom spoke to the bird and said, "We mean you no harm. A whale left us in the Land of Trees. And we knew no way to get out unless you took us. Carry us to the river Zool, and I'll tickle you no more."

When the bird heard these words, he was pleased. He said, "That's easy. As you wish, so shall it be done. I'll take you to the Zool river to-night."

After that, each did as he had agreed. Noom-Zor-Noom put away his wand and stopped tickling the bird's toes. And the Mellikanoo stretched out his long neck, cried, "Mellikanoo-kanooo-kanoooooooooooo," and started off in the direction of the river Zool.

All that night the bird flew through the sky, carrying the golden basket with him. Noom-Zor-Noom lifted Tal up on to the edge of the basket and held him there while he sat with his feet dangling over the edge. They went so close to the moon that Tal waved to the man in the moon and shouted, "Hello!"

And the man in the moon smiled and said, "Hello, Tal. Where are you going?"

"To Troom," said Tal. "How did you know my name?"

"I know every child's name," said the man. "I watch over them at night."

"Not every night," said Tal.

"No," said the man. "Some nights I don't look at all. Other nights I peep over the edge of the sky with part of my face. Then sometimes I think it best to take a good, big look. Then you see all my face."

"That's a full moon, isn't it?" asked Tal.

"A what?" asked the man, looking surprised.

"A full moon," said Tal. "That's what we call it, anyhow."

"So that's what they call me, when I look down on them," the man muttered. He thought for a moment, then said, "Will you spell that for me? I'm not sure I understood what you said."

"F-U-L-L M-O . . ." began Tal. But before he had time to finish, he had passed by the moon and could talk to the man no more.

Then they flew near to many of the stars. And all of a sudden they flew into what seemed like a fog. Only it was different from most fogs, for the air was filled with thousands of little diamond specks that sparkled and glistened with their own light. This was the Milky Way. After they had passed through it, Noom-Zor-Noom gathered up all the specks that had fallen into the basket. With great care he put them into a silver box and gave it to Tal. He said, "You keep this. It will come in handy some day."

"Will they always shine?" asked Tal, taking the box.

"Always," said the old man. "Be careful not to lose it."

"I'd better leave it in the basket," said Tal. "I might drop it now." And he handed it back to Noom-Zor-Noom, who set it down where it would be safe.

They passed by a small comet; and the old man caught hold of it and gave it to Tal to play with. He held it by its tail and swung it around so that it made a great circle of light. Then he let it go and watched it disappear in the distance. So they went on through the sky, flying in and out among the stars. Not once during the whole night did they stop, nor did they see the earth at all.

In the morning, just as the sun was lighting up the sky, and the stars, one after the other, were closing their eyes and going to sleep, the Mellikanoo began to circle down toward the earth. Down and down he went in great circles, until Tal looked over the edge of the basket and could see land. The land was flat, like a great plain; and through the middle of the plain ran a river. When they came nearer to the earth, Tal saw that the river was bright green. He turned to Noom-Zor-Noom and said, "What's that river below us? I have never seen a river that was such bright green."

"That's the Zool," said Noom-Zor-Noom. "It's all liquid jade, that's why it's so green."

The next minute the Mellikanoo swooped down so close to the river that the bottom of the basket rested on the water. But the bird still stayed in the air, he did not come down. He flew slowly towards the shore and dragged the basket in so close that it touched the land. Then he turned his head and said, "I have done as I promised I would. Here you are on the shore of the river Zool. Now will you please untie me?"

"I will," said Noom-Zor-Noom; and he reached up and untied the rope from the bird's legs.

As soon as his legs were free, the Mellikanoo settled down on the water beside the basket. He stuck his head

over the edge and asked, "Who is this boy, and where is
he going?"

"I am taking him to Troom," said Noom-Zor-Noom.

"I have heard of that country," said the Mellikanoo,
"but I have never been there. It's a long way off, isn't
it?"

"Yes," said Noom-Zor-Noom. Then he went on and
told the bird how far they had come, and how they had
traveled across the sea in a whale's stomach.

After the old man had finished talking, Tal turned to
the Mellikanoo and said, "These feathers that the basket
is made of belong to you. Wouldn't you like them
back?"

The Mellikanoo was pleased with these words: he answered and said, "Thank you for thinking of it, but
really they are of no use to me. And they may be of
great use to you. You keep them."

"Thank you," said Tal. "Isn't there anything we can
do for you?"

"No," said the bird. "I must be going." He swam
off a short distance from the basket, and there he
stopped to drink his fill of green water. After doing
that, he flew away and was soon out of sight in the sky.

When the Mellikanoo had gone, Noom-Zor-Noom
said, "This river rises in the mountains near Troom.
Here we must stay until a boat comes by and picks us
up, for we have neither oars nor sails. We'll have to
get a boat to tow us."

Because they had been up all night, the three of them were tired. So they lay down in the bottom of the golden basket and went to sleep. They did not wake up until late in the afternoon. Then Noom-Zor-Noom said, "I must read you another story. Otherwise there will not be enough time for you to hear them all. You must hear every one, for whether I shall go to prison or not depends on which one you choose." He uncovered the crystal block and read Tal the story about

TRUMBILLOO, THE MAGICIAN

TRUMBILLOO was a magician. He lived in a cave in the side of a hill. The cave was not cold and dark: it was all fixed up in a marvelous way. The walls were made of dark blue stone, and glowed as if there were a light behind them. The ceiling was shiny black with here and there a crystal star that twinkled like a real one. And on the floor the magician had a rug made of nothing but pearls. Just thousands and thousands of them all woven together with silver threads.

Trumbilloo was a funny little man. He wore shoes with pointed, turned-up toes. The shoes were gold, and out of the toe of each one shot a flame—an orange flame out of the right and a green flame out of the left. His suit was of soft velvet and changed color according to his wish. Now it was blue, now red, now yellow. On his head he wore a tiny peaked cap that gave forth a perfume like the sweetest rose in the world.

All day and all night Trumbilloo lived in his cave. He never went out, and no one ever went in to see him. Yet people knew he was there, for every now and then at night they would sneak up to the door of his cave and peep in. Then they would go back home and tell of the wonderful sights they had seen. How the magician had changed pebbles into jewels. How he had made a little marble figure come to life. How they had seen a little girl with him one night, and the next thing they saw was the little girl changed into a bird. The bird was like no other bird in the world. It sat on Trumbilloo's shoulder, sang to him, and every time his suit changed color the bird also changed. Such were the things people saw in the cave, but no one dared go in.

One night a boy, who had heard much about Trumbilloo, decided to go into his cave. He never said a word to his mother and father about what he was going to do. But, after he had been in bed for a long time, and everybody in the house was sound asleep, he climbed out at the window and ran off to see the magician. When he came to the cave, he knocked at the door. Trumbilloo said, "Tell me who you are and come in."

The boy said, "My name is Zan." And he walked in.

Trumbilloo, seeing the boy, said, "Why do you come here at this hour of the night? No one has ever come into my cave. Yet you dare to come in the middle of the night."

Zan said, "I have heard such-and-such and such-and-such about you. Now I have come to see whether you can really do these things or not. Can you make a marble figure come to life? Can you change a person into a bird? If you'd like to show me some of these things, I'd like to see them. If not, I'll go back."

Trumbilloo liked the way the boy spoke. So he said, "I can do all these things and more. Tell me what you want to see, and I'll show it to you."

The boy said, "I want to see a marble figure come to life."

At that, the magician walked over and opened a silver door in the wall. He reached in and took out a marble figure of a boy about the size of Zan. Then he went to the back of the cave and stood the figure on a table. And he said to Zan, "Watch! Keep your eyes open and don't be afraid."

With these words that the magician spoke, the cave became dark. For a minute nothing happened. Then the flames that came out of Trumbilloo's shoes began to get brighter and brighter and brighter. Soon the orange and green light was so dazzling that Zan could see nothing, even though he tried to keep his eyes open. After this the flames died down; the cave lit up with a mysterious blue light; and on the table Zan saw a little boy.

But the magician was nowhere to be seen. So scared was Zan, that he was about to run out of the cave, when the boy spoke to him, "Don't go away, Zan. If you stay, you'll see a lot more. Now I'm going to be changed into a dog."

Again the cave became dark. In the darkness Zan thought he saw all kinds of things. Little sparks of light of every color seemed to float in the air, and there was a strong smell of roses. At last the blue light came on again. Trumbilloo was standing near the table, and on the table was a dog. The magician whistled, the dog jumped off the table and ran to Zan. Trumbilloo said, "There's a dog for you. You can take him home if you wish."

Zan was so surprised at all he had seen, that he could not speak. He just stood there patting the dog and looking at the magician. Finally he said, "You have changed that little boy into an animal. Could you change me into one?"

Trumbilloo said, "I can change you into any kind of an animal you wish. Tell me, and I'll do it."

Zan thought. Often he had wished to become an animal; but now that the chance was at hand, he could not make up his mind which one it would be. He thought to himself, "A dog has a nice life. It runs in the fields all day, and at night it sleeps by the fire. But perhaps it would be more fun to be a wild animal. I don't want to be a horse or a donkey: they have to work too hard." And in his mind he ran over every possible animal he could think of. Then he said to the magician, "I think I'd like tc be a frog."

"Why a frog?" asked Trumbilloo. "That's a stupid animal to be."

But the boy insisted that he would rather be a frog than anything else. He wanted to be able to sit by a pool all day and dive and swim. And in the evening he could croak, and make a noise just like all the other frogs. These things he told the magician, and Trumbilloo said, "Since that's what you wish, it shall be done. But you must make up your mind to do whatever I say. If you don't, my magic may not work, and you won't become a frog."

So Zan promised to do everything he was told. And Trumbilloo made ready to turn him into a frog.

First he lit a fire in a golden brazier. After it was burning well, he took out a long, slender pipe. He dipped the bowl of the pipe into a pot of liquid he had near him, and then he started to blow. His little cheeks puffed up until it seemed they would burst. Finally, out of the bowl of the pipe, a bubble started to grow. It grew and grew, the harder he blew, and did not stop growing until it was big enough to hold the boy. Then the magician held it over the fire, and the flames ran into the glass bubble and danced just as if the whole thing were ablaze. But it could not have been hot, for Trumbilloo lifted it off the pipe with his own hands and carried it over to the table. After setting it down very carefully, he said, "Come, step up on the table and walk into the bubble."

Zan looked at him in surprise. How could he walk into a glass bubble without breaking it? Anyhow, he did as the magician told him. He climbed up on to the table, and, with his hands in front of his eyes, he stepped right through the glass. Nothing happened. Nothing broke. He found himself inside a large sphere, and he was entirely surrounded by dancing flames. Still he could hear the voice of the magician, who was saying, "Are you in? Do as I tell you!"

Zan said, "I'm in. What are you going to do to me?"

Trumbilloo said, "Sit down and hold your knees in your arms."

After that Zan heard nothing more. Very slowly the glass sphere started to turn. At first so slowly that he could hardly notice it; but always it kept going a little faster. Round and round it went. Soon it was spinning as fast as a top. Zan tried to keep from getting dizzy. All he could see were flames rushing by him at a terrific speed. He made an effort to shout, but his voice had left him. Finally things grew black, and he remembered nothing more.

The next morning, just as the sun was coming up, Zan found himself on a big rock at the edge of a pool. He tried to speak, and all he could do was croak. For he was no longer a boy but a frog. The sun felt very warm and very nice. So he gave a hop and dived into the water. "This is great fun," he thought, "to be able to swim as well as this." All that day he did nothing but swim and lie on the rock in the sun. He was glad to be a frog and spend all his time in the water.

The day passed, evening came. After the sun had gone down, the water began to get cold. So the frog hopped out on to the rock, but it was cold too. He looked around for a warm spot, but could find none. He thought, "What am I to do? I can't stay here and be cold all night."

He left the pool and started to hop home. When he got there, though he croaked and croaked for all he was worth, no one paid any attention to him. And he had to spend the night out in the garden under a cabbage leaf.

All the frog wished for now was to be changed back to a boy again. But how this could be done, he did not know. He could not remember how to get to the magician. And even if he had, he never could have hopped up the hill. However, he did have a feeling that if some one would call him by his own name, the spell would be broken. So he hopped up to the house and put his head in at the door. His mother was sitting there sewing. When she saw the frog, she called to her husband and said, "Here's a frog. What do you think he has come here for?"

The frog said, "Chugger-runk, chugger-runk, chugger-runk."

The old man said, "The garden is full of them. They come out of that pool over there. Give him to me, and I'll throw him back." So he picked up the frog, carried him back to the pool, and threw him in.

Again the frog hopped back to the house and sat by the door and croaked, "Chugger-runk, chugger-runk, chugger-runk."

Just then it happened that the boy's mother dropped her needle. The frog hopped in, picked up the needle, and jumped up on to the woman's lap with it. The woman said, "You are a nice frog. Stay here with me and I'll feed you."

The father, when he heard what the frog had done, thought it all foolishness. He said, "Don't keep that frog here. He will only be a nuisance." But the mother insisted, and she kept the frog in the house and fed him well.

After a while they both came to like the frog very much, and they wanted to give him a name. But they could think of none. The woman said, "He is so nice and kind. Why don't we name him after our boy, who has gone?"

The man said, "You don't want to name a frog after our son. That wouldn't be right."

The frog went, "Chugger-runk, chugger-runk, chugger-runk."

The man and the woman could not agree. So they did not name the frog.

The frog stayed with them and lived in a bucket of water in the kitchen. Later on they again talked about naming him. And the frog made such a noise and jumped around so, that the woman became suspicious. She said, "See! Whenever we talk about naming him, he is very happy. I think he is some one that has been turned into a frog. I am going to name him." She picked the frog out of the bucket and looked into his eyes. And the frog began to cry and said, "Chugger-runk."

"I don't care what you say," said the mother. "I am going to name him Zan." She looked at the frog and said, "Zan!" No sooner had she said it, than the frog turned into a boy; and in her arms the old woman was holding her own son.

Then Zan told her all about what had happened to him. And his mother was sorry that she had not given the frog a name long before.

"IT WASN'T her fault," said Tal. "I don't blame her for not wanting to name a frog after her boy."

"Nobody said it was her fault," said Millitinkle, who had been asleep during most of the story, but was now sitting on her hind legs rubbing her sleepy eyes with her hooves. "Nobody said anything about that. Why didn't you listen to the story?"

"I did," said Tal. He spoke crossly, for he saw no reason for the donkey's words. "You're the one that didn't listen."

"Yes, I did," said the donkey.

"You were asleep," said Tal, triumphantly. "You just woke up." And to himself he thought that at last he had got the best of Millitinkle.

"But I can hear in my sleep," said the donkey. "That's why I'm better off than you."

Tal's jaw dropped, and his eyes opened wide. For a while he did not say anything, he just looked at Noom-Zor-Noom. Then he asked, "Is that true, Noom-Zor-Noom?"

"If Millitinkle says so, it must be," said the old man. "She knows."

"But you know that I was listening to the story," said Tal. "Wasn't I?"

"Yes," said the old man.

"Then Millitinkle had no right to say what she did," continued Tal. "I don't care whether she can hear in her sleep or not. She shouldn't have said I wasn't listening. You tell her so."

"She was just having some fun with you," said the old man, smiling. "You mustn't mind that. It's her way of having a good time."

"But I don't like it," insisted Tal. "I don't want you to think I wasn't listening, when I was."

"I know you were," said Noom-Zor-Noom. "So don't

worry about that. And don't be bothered about what Millitinkle says. She loves to argue. I can make her stop, if you want me to. But you wouldn't like to spoil her fun, would you?"

Tal looked at Millitinkle. And as he looked, she smiled and winked at him and made the little golden bells tinkle. And Tal laughed to himself and thought what a wonderful donkey she really was. He turned to the old man and said, "No: don't stop her. She can argue with me all she wants."

CHAPTER X

THE HOME OF THE WIMZIES AND THE STORY
OF SAR, NAR, AND JINOOK

WHILE they were sitting on the shore of the jade river that evening, a boat suddenly came into sight. It was a beautiful boat all made out of turquoise with red sails the color of wine. It moved up the river slowly, for there was not much wind to blow it along. When it came near to where Noom-Zor-Noom and Tal were sitting, the old man got up and shouted at the top of his lungs. The captain of the boat heard him and turned in toward shore. And pretty soon the boat was so close to land that Noom-Zor-Noom was able to speak to the captain. He said, "We have been left here by a bird. This basket is our boat. But we have no oars and we have no sail. If you are going up the river and will take us along, you will be doing us a great favor."

The captain said, "I am going as far as the waterfalls. Beyond that place no one goes. If you wish to come, I shall be glad to take you." And he brought his boat to shore.

Then Noom-Zor-Noom thanked the captain. And he and Tal and Millitinkle got on board. They tied the golden basket out behind. And in that way they started up the Zool river.

This boat that they went on was loaded with pebbles; that was all: there was nothing else on board. And when Tal saw so many pebbles, he said to the captain, "Why have you got all these pebbles on board? Where are you going with them?"

The captain said, "This cargo of pebbles is going up to the Wimzies, who live under the waterfalls. The Wimzies take the pebbles and coat them with jade in a way that only they know. After the pebbles have been coated, I take them back and sell them for beads to make necklaces."

"Who are the Wimzies?" asked Tal. "I've never heard of them before. Where do they live, and what do they look like?"

"They are little people that live up behind the water-falls," said the captain. "You'll see what they look like when we get there. It's better that I shouldn't try to describe them, because they don't look like any other people."

"Are they big or small?" asked Tal, who was curious to know more.

"Small," said the captain. "But don't ask me any more questions. You'll see them to-morrow."

That night they slept on the turquoise boat. And in the morning Noom-Zor-Noom went to the captain and said, "You have been kind enough to take us along without pay. Tell me, is there anything I can do for you?"

"Yes," said the captain. "If you don't mind telling me, I should like to know who you are and from what place you come."

"My name is Noom-Zor-Noom," said the old man. "My home is in Troom. Have you ever heard of that place?"

"Yes," said the captain. "I have heard it spoken of, but I have never been there. I didn't know that any one ever left that place."

"Sometimes we do," said the old man. And he went on and told the captain why he had been traveling all over the world. He told him about Tal and Millitinkle, and he showed him how the donkey could talk. When the captain heard all this and saw what kind of passengers he had on board, he was glad that he had taken them along. He said, "Indeed I am fortunate to have you on board. In all the years that I have been on this river, I have never met any one like you. I, myself, love a good story better than anything else. If you will read me one of yours, I shall feel more than repaid for what I have done. So if you wish to, read me one. If not, don't."

"That's easy," said Noom-Zor-Noom. "You ask for little in return for all the trouble we have caused you. I have a long story that I think you will like. If you have time, I shall read it to you."

"I have," said the captain.

With these words that the captain spoke, Noom-Zor-Noom got up and uncovered the crystal block. Then he made Tal sit down and listen, while he started to read the captain the story of

SAR, NAR, AND JINOOK

THERE were three brothers who lived in a village with their mother. Their names were Sar, Nar, and Jinook. Sar and Nar were much older than Jinook; and Jinook was lame, he had a crooked leg. Even though he was lame, he was the one who did all the work. Sar and Nar played all day and had a good time, while Jinook stayed at home and helped his mother. When he did play, he had only such toys as his brothers had cast aside. He never had any new clothes, because he always wore the ones that had become too small for Sar and Nar. And he hardly ever went outside, for he was ashamed of being lame and different from other boys.

Time passed; Sar, Nar, and Jinook grew up. Sar became sixteen, Nar fourteen, and Jinook was only ten. One night when they were all sitting at home, they heard a feeble rapping at the door. Then the door opened, and an old man came in. He was tired and thin, and his shoes were all worn out from walking. He said, "I am old, and I have come far. Will you let me spend the night in your house?"

Sar said, "We are poor, and all we have is what you see. We have no bed for you. Nor can we give you anything to eat."

Nar said, "There is an inn at the next village. If you go there, you can get a place to sleep and can buy yourself some food."

After these two brothers had spoken, Jinook said, "My bed is small, but you may have it to-night. I shall sleep on the floor. If my brothers won't give you food, you can have my supper." And he welcomed the old man and invited him in.

When Sar and Nar saw how kind Jinook was, they were ashamed of themselves. At once they begged the old man to spend the night, saying that they would give him anything he wanted. So he came in, and they treated him the way an old man should be treated. They cooked a large supper, and all sat down and ate. After supper the stranger said, "You have treated me well. If you wish, I'll tell you a story."

"We'd love to hear one," said the boys.

So the old man began:

"Far, far away there is a country where only animals live. As there are no men to be cruel to them, all the animals are very happy. They talk and live just like men; and they do only what they wish. The donkeys have no loads to carry, the horses no carts to draw, and the oxen no plows to drag. Even the wild beasts are tame and go about peacefully among all the other animals.

"Once a cat that lived in this kingdom of animals got lost, he could not find his way home. So he wandered and wandered until he wandered far away into a strange land. The land that he came into was ruled by a cruel king. When the cat came there, one of the king's servants caught him and took him to the palace. The king, seeing how beautiful the cat was, kept him for himself. He ordered his men to feed the cat on milk and meat and everything else that was good.

"After a while the cat tired of so much good food. He thought to himself, 'It is very fine of the king to feed me so well. But it is easy for him to give freely of such things as money can buy. It would be better if he fed me less and paid me more attention. This he cannot do, for his heart is hard. He has never petted me, he has never spoken a kind word to me, he has never even taken

me up in his lap.   Instead he teases me and scolds me;
and often he loses his temper and beats me cruelly for
things I have never done.   I don't like to live with such
a man.   If he can't love me with his heart, why does he
bother with me at all?   He can keep his food, I don't
want it.' So the cat was unhappy.   He avoided the king
as much as possible, and spent most of his time seeking
some way out of the palace.

"Now this king had a big garden.   And at the end of
the big garden, near the palace, was a little garden all
walled in with a high stone wall.   No door opened into
this little garden; and no one knew what grew inside,
for there was only one way of looking in, that was from
a small window in the king's bedroom.   But no one
dared look out of this window, for fear of having his
head chopped off.   So the secret of the little garden remained unknown to all but the king himself.

"That the little garden did hold a secret was admitted
by all who lived in the palace.   Some said that the king
had a treasure there, buried under the roots of a tree.
Some thought that the whole garden was filled with
gold pieces.   Others said that bins packed with jewels
were kept there.   Different as these stories were, all
agreed on this point: that in the little garden the king
had something that was the source of great, great wealth.
For otherwise where did all his money come from?

"The cat had not been in the palace long, before he
too became curious about the little garden.   So one night

he crept into the king's room and hid under the bed, hoping for a chance to look out of the window. But no sooner had he got into the room, than he was seized with fright and did not dare go to the window. So he stayed under the bed and waited. The king came to bed. In the middle of the night he got up, dressed, and went into the corner of the room, where he slid back one of the great stones in the wall. Then he disappeared, and the cat could hear him tiptoeing down a long flight of stairs. With a bound the cat was up on the window-sill, and there, in the little garden, he saw the king. He was walking around picking fruit off a tree that looked like a big apple tree. When the king had picked an armful of fruit, he left the garden and started back up the stairs. But before he reached the room, the cat opened the door and ran down the hall just as fast as he could. So really he did not see what kind of fruit it was that the king had in his arms.

"For days and days the cat could think of nothing but the little garden. He was not so interested in the fruit, as he was in the tree. Because he knew, that if he could get down into the garden, climb the tree, and jump to the wall, there might be some hope of his escaping. He thought and thought about it, until he made up his mind to try. After that he was somewhat happier, for he felt that he would not have to put up with the king's cruelty much longer.

"One day the king had been more cruel than ever to

his cat. He had beaten him and kicked him and even gone so far as to twist his tail to make him scream. The cat, who was no longer able to bear such treatment, decided to run away that night. So again he hid under the king's bed, and there he waited for his chance to get to the garden. As was his custom, the king got up in the middle of the night and opened the stone in the wall. The cat waited until he could hear the king's footsteps no more, then he sneaked down the stairs and out into the garden. And before the king knew what was happening, the cat climbed up the tree and ran out on one of the branches. There he stopped long enough to bite off a small sprig. The next minute he leaped, landed on top of the wall, and bounded out of sight. So he ran away from the king. And the king was sorry he had not treated the cat better.

"The cat ran and ran and ran. He never stopped, until one day he found himself back in the Kingdom of the Animals. What he did with the sprig, no one knows for certain. But it is believed that he planted it, and that it grew into a tree just like the one in the king's garden. People think this because in a few years the Kingdom of the Animals became very rich, much richer than it had ever been before. And the only way to explain this would be that the cat planted the sprig that he stole from the little garden, and that the sprig grew into just such a tree as was the source of all the king's wealth.

"Word of how rich all the animals were came to the

ears of the cruel king.   When he heard it, he sent army
after army to try to conquer the Kingdom of the Animals.   But always these armies were beaten by the wild
animals, until the king lost so many men that he had to
give up the fight.

"Since then few men have started for the Kingdom of
the Animals to look for the tree.   Only two or three have
ever found the kingdom.   And of those who got there,
none have seen the tree.   But probably it is still there,
waiting for the right person to pick a sprig off it.   All
the animals guard it closely and do not like to have people trying to find it.   So perhaps it's just as well that
more men have not set out to go to the Kingdom of the
Animals."

Thus the old man spoke.   And when he had finished
his story, Sar asked, "Is it really true that there's such a
place?   How much money do you suppose there is in
the tree?"

The old man said, "That I don't know.   But I do
know that there is such a place."

Nar asked, "If I picked a sprig, could I plant it and
become rich?"

"Yes," said the old man.

Then the two older boys asked how to get there, and
the old man told them.   They asked how much money
they could make and what the tree was like.   And all
they could think of was the fortune that would be theirs
if they found the tree.

But Jinook remained silent, he said nothing. His mind was full of thoughts about the animals. He wanted to see them, talk to them, and live for a while in their kingdom. Whether he found the tree or not, made little difference; but with all his heart he longed to see the animals. To him that would be much more fun than finding a lot of money.

That night the old man slept in the house, and early the next morning he went away. No sooner had he gone, than Sar and Nar talked of setting out to find the tree. Jinook wanted to go with them as far as the Kingdom of the Animals; but they laughed at him and said, "How could you go? You are small and lame. We could not be bothered taking you along with us. If we go, you must stay here with Mother." And they bragged and boasted about how strong they were and how they could do what no one else had ever done before. Finally their mother got so tired of hearing them talk, that she told them to go. She made them each a new suit and gave each a strong pair of shoes. Then she prepared food for them to have on the way, and she sent them off with her blessing. And they left home in high spirits, promising to come back with all the riches in the world.

Jinook stayed with his mother. A year passed, and no word came from Sar and Nar. It was the spring of the second year, when one day Jinook was out in the fields blowing soap bubbles. He had a beautiful big pipe that belonged to Sar; and the bubbles he blew were almost as big as Jinook himself. As they drifted away in the breeze, he ran after them as best he could, laughing and singing all the time, for he had never been so happy. Finally he decided to see how big a bubble he could blow. He dipped his pipe in the soapsuds and blew and blew with all his might. He blew so hard, that before he knew it he blew himself right through the stem of the pipe and into the soap bubble. When he looked out he saw the fields and trees sinking away below him. Thousands of rainbows seemed to be dancing all around. Higher and higher he went, until his own house was just a speck on the ground. Then he saw a lot of mountains slowly drift by and fade in the distance. Soon he was out over the blue sea, and in every direction he looked he saw nothing but water. All the time the big soap bubble was rocking back and forth like a cradle. This made Jinook sleepy; he could stay awake no longer. So he curled up in the bottom of the bubble, closed his eyes, and went to sleep.

ALL THE TIME that Noom-Zor-Noom had been reading the story, the sound of the distant waterfalls had been getting louder and louder. By the time he reached the part where Jinook went to sleep in the bubble, the roar of the waterfalls was so loud, that the old man could not make his voice heard above it. So he stopped reading and said, "There's no use of my reading any more. There's too much noise."

The captain said, "That's a good story. I wish you could finish it."

"I can't," said Noom-Zor-Noom. "Not now."

Hardly had he spoken these words and put away the crystal block, when the ship rounded a bend in the river, and there, right ahead of them, were the falls. They were higher than any waterfalls in the world. And the cliff that the jade water fell over was made of rock as black as ink. For a while Tal looked at it in amazement, then he said, "I like those falls. But where are the Wimzies?"

The captain shouted, "Look in the water, and you'll see them."

Tal did as the captain told him. He looked into the water near the falls, and there he saw thousands of little people. Their bodies were bluish green, and their heads looked exactly like little bubbles. They were swimming and turning somersaults in the water; and every now and then some of them would climb out on the rocks and dive back in.

"I've never seen any people like them before," said Tal. "Don't they do anything but swim and dive in the river?"

"That's all they do in the daytime," said the captain. "They love nothing better than that. At night they go to their houses and work coating pebbles with jade."

"Where are their houses?" asked Tal.

"In the cliff behind the falls," said the captain. "You'll see them in a minute."

The boat sailed around one end of the falls and went in behind them. Then everything became green, for all the light was colored by the water that it shone through. Behind the falls was a wide, deep pool that ran along the foot of the cliff. It was in this cliff that the Wimzies lived. Each of them had a little hole in the rock, and each hole had a little golden door that opened and shut with a latch. In front of the rows of holes were ledges wide enough to stand on; and in the rock were cut steps, leading from each ledge to the one above. The whole face of the cliff back of the falls was covered with rows of holes and ledges. In all there must have been ten thousand Wimzie houses.

Alongside this cliff the ship stopped. The captain and his men got out, and they went from hole to hole. They reached into each hole and took out a handful of jade-coated pebbles. And in their place they put a handful of ordinary pebbles. All day long they worked without stopping. And Tal and Noom-Zor-Noom helped. By night all the pebbles from the boat had been exchanged for jade beads. Then the captain said, "We must be going. I don't dare stay here after dark. Do you wish to go back with us?"

"No, thanks," said Noom-Zor-Noom. "We'll stay here. But how about the rest of the story?"

"I'd like to hear it," said the captain. "But I haven't got time. It's late now. And unless we get out from here before dark, we shan't be able to find our way down the river."

"Don't let us keep you," said Noom-Zor-Noom. "Just leave us anywhere here."

So the captain sailed over to where there was a flat rock, and there he left Tal, Noom-Zor-Noom, and Milli-tinkle with their golden basket. After he was certain that he could do nothing more for them, he sailed out from behind the falls and went away.

As soon as the boat had left, Noom-Zor-Noom took Tal to another part of the cliff, where the captain had not been. There, at the foot of the cliff, he showed him three big holes that looked like caves. Out of each one a river of green water was pouring into the pool behind the falls. Noom-Zor-Noom looked at them and said, "We must go up one of those underground rivers. One of them leads to Troom, but I don't know which. The other two go to places from which no man has ever returned."

"How will we find out which is the right one?" asked Tal. "I'd hate to go up the wrong one. And how are we going to get up it?"

Noom-Zor-Noom said, "The Wimzies know. If we are nice to them, they will tell. They will even pull us up in our golden basket. If they won't tell us, we must stay here."

"You mean we'll never get to Troom?" said Tal. "I wouldn't like that."

"We'll get there all right," said Noom-Zor-Noom. "It's just a matter of time."

Then they went back to the flat rock and sat down to wait until evening came. For as soon as the sun began to set, the Wimzies always left the water and came back to their homes in the rock cliff behind the falls.

CHAPTER XI

*THE UNDERGROUND RIVER AND THE STORY
OF SAR, NAR, AND JINOOK* (*Continued*)

WHILE they were sitting on the rock waiting for the Wimzies to come home, Tal said, "Read me the rest of the story of Sar, Nar, and Jinook."

"How far did we get?" asked the old man.

"To the place where Jinook had fallen asleep in the bottom of the soap bubble. What happened after that? Did he go to the land where all the animals live?"

Noom-Zor-Noom did not answer. A strange sadness had overcome him. He sat as if in a dream, his wide-open eyes gazing without expression into the distance. His forehead was wrinkled, and now and then he shook his head as if in despair. When Tal looked at him, he too felt sad, for he knew that something was troubling the old man. He said, "I know you're worried about something. What's the matter?"

"Nothing," said the old man.

"There's something," said Tal. "And I know what it is. You're worrying about that old Door and going to prison. Aren't you?" And when Noom-Zor-Noom did not answer him, he went on and said, "You can open that Door. You can do anything. Any of the stories

158

you've told me will do it. I won't let King Tazzarin put you in prison. I'll kick and pound the Door, until it has to come open."

"That's all very well," said Noom-Zor-Noom. "But you won't be able to come into Troom."

"Why not?" asked Tal. "Who's going to stop me?"

"The guards at the gate," said the old man.

"I'll get by them somehow," said Tal. "I'm not going to let you go in alone. Something might happen to you, and I wouldn't be there to help you."

"We'll think about that later," said Noom-Zor-Noom.

"You always want to think about things later," said Tal. "Won't you say that you are going to take me in?"

"I can't," said the old man. "There's nothing I'd rather do than take you with me. But it's not for me to decide."

"What will you do with me then?" asked Tal.

"I'll have to leave you outside," said the old man. "You'll be safe there."

"I don't want to be safe," said Tal. "I want to go with you."

"I know you do," said the old man, cheering up. "Let's not think of that now. It's more important that you should hear my stories. The first thing you have to do is to choose one of them. You can help me more that way than any other."

"Anyhow, I'm going to think there's a chance of my going into Troom," said Tal. "I can do that, can't I?"

"Yes," said the old man. "There's always a chance."

"And it's a big chance, isn't it?" added Tal, looking at the old man hopefully.

Noom-Zor-Noom did not say another word. He got up and walked over to where the crystal block was. There he sat down and began to read the rest of the story of Sar, Nar, and Jinook. This is how it went:

WHEN Jinook woke up, he was floating along near the ground. As he looked down, he saw a broad stretch of grass barely out of reach below him. Then something happened: there was a pop, the bubble burst, and Jinook found himself lying in the middle of a field. He looked for the soap bubble, it had disappeared into thin air. He looked all around, and in every direction he saw nothing but woods and hills. So he got up and started to walk. After a while he came to a road that ran along the edge of a small stream. This road he took, and he followed it as far as it went. At the end of the road he came to a house. When he knocked at the door, a spider opened it and asked, "Who are you, and what do you want?"

Jinook spoke kindly and said, "Such-and-such happened to me. I blew myself inside a soap bubble, and it carried me here. Now, can you tell me where I am? How far am I from home?"

The spider said, "You are in a land where nothing but animals live. Are you sure you have come in search of nothing?"

"I didn't even know I was coming," said Jinook. "But I have heard of this place. And I have always wanted to come just to live with the animals. I love animals and am always kind to them."

After the spider made certain that Jinook was not searching for the tree, she invited him in. She gave him a piece of bread and a bowl of milk. Then she said, "It's good that you are kind to animals. Otherwise it would not be safe for you to be here. We animals do not like to have men visit our kingdom. Only last year a boy came and said to me, 'Where is the tree that holds the secret of wealth?' And when I told him I didn't know, he threatened to kill me. So I made him a prisoner, and he is still here."

When she spoke these words, Jinook knew that she was talking of one of his brothers. He asked, "Where is that boy?"

The spider took him into the back yard, and there was Sar all tangled up in a huge web that was spun between two trees. The more he struggled to free himself, the more tangled he became. His back was toward Jinook, so he did not see him. The spider laughed and said, "Once a year our king, the lion, judges all the prisoners. If he thinks fit, they are freed and sent back home. If not, they stay prisoners forever. It depends on how cruel they have been. Until the lion comes here, that boy must stay as he is."

Jinook was sad. He did not tell the spider who Sar

was. But he made up his mind to find the lion and beg mercy for his brother. So he asked, "Where does your king, the lion, live?"

The spider said, "Go back by the road you have come. Then take such-and-such a road. You will have to travel a long way. I don't think you should go so far into our kingdom. Here you are safe; but I don't know how the animals will treat you further on."

Jinook thanked the spider for all she had done. He left the house and came back on the road by the stream. Then he found the road that the spider had spoken of. He went as far as it went, and he came to another house. This house belonged to an ant, who lived there with his wife and children. The ant was out in the fields working. But his wife was at home cooking food for her thousand children. When Jinook came to the door she asked, "Who are you and what do you want?" He told her the same as he had told the spider. And she asked him the same questions. Then he went in and helped her with the cooking. After all the children had eaten, the ant said, "You are not like other men I have seen."

Jinook said, "Why do you say that?"

The ant said, "Last year a boy came here. He looked something like you. He said to me, 'Where is the tree that holds the secret of all wealth?' When I told him that I did not know, he became angry and said, 'You *do* know. You just don't want to tell me. Either tell me,

THE SPIDER TOOK HIM INTO THE BACK YARD, AND THERE WAS SAR ALL TANGLED UP IN A HUGE WEB THAT WAS SPUN BETWEEN TWO TREES.

or I'll crush you under my heel.' And he would have killed me, had not my husband and all my children made him prisoner. Come, I'll show you where he is."

She led Jinook to the back door; and there, out in the yard, he saw Nar buried up to his neck in a huge ant-hill. Nar was asleep, so he did not see his brother. Jinook asked, "How long will that boy stay there?"

"Until our king, the lion, comes and gives judgment," said the ant. "Then that boy may be freed, or he may stay there forever."

Again Jinook was sad. He asked the ant all about the lion and how to get to his house. She told him a great deal, much more than the spider had told him. So Jinook set out to find the lion and beg mercy for his brothers. For many months he took this road and that road, until finally he came to a palace. He walked up the front steps and knocked at the door. This palace was the home of the lion, the king of all the animals. When the lion heard that a lame boy had come to see him, he ordered his servants to put the boy in a room by himself and give him all he wanted to eat. After Jinook had rested and eaten, the lion went in to him. He said, "I have heard all about you. You have been very good to my people. You have done none of them harm. Tell me what you want."

Jinook trembled with fear. He was afraid of the lion, and he was ashamed to tell him about Sar and Nar.

He said, "I have come to ask a favor of you. But I am ashamed to say what it is."

The lion said, "Tell me, that I may grant it."

Then Jinook told him all about his brothers, what had happened to them. He asked the lion to forgive them and let them go home. The lion listened but said nothing. He went out of the room and into another room. In that room he took off his lion skin and became an old man, the same old man that had told the story about the cat. Then he came back to the boy. When Jinook saw the old man, he did not know what to say, for he could not believe his eyes.

"Do you know me?" asked the old man.

"Yes," said Jinook. "But how can you be both a lion and an old man?"

The old man said, "In the kingdom of men I am an old man, in the kingdom of animals I am a lion." And he went out and put on his lion skin again. He came back as a lion and said, "You treated me well at your house. Now I shall treat you well here. Your brothers did not treat me well, so you see what has happened to them. For your sake I will free them, but not yet. You must stay here with me for a while. I have something to show you." So Jinook stayed in the lion's palace and was happy.

One day the lion said, "Get on my back and ride. We are going for a trip."

Jinook climbed up on the lion's back and held on to

his mane. The lion walked out of the palace and went off through the village. All the animals when they saw Jinook spoke to him and shook his hand. They greeted him and asked him to stay in their kingdom as long as he wished. On through the village they went, and for many days they traveled through a forest. Jinook saw many wonderful sights such as he had never seen before. At last they came to a big lake. Without stopping, the lion walked into the water and swam across with the boy on his back. There, on the other side of the lake, they went up the side of a steep hill to where there was a cave. The lion said, "Don't be afraid. As long as you are with me you will be safe." So they went into the cave. No sooner had they entered, than Jinook heard the most terrible sounds, as if all the animals in the world were talking at once. The lion shouted, "Silence, here comes the king!" As he spoke, all the noise stopped, and suddenly the cave was lit up with millions of lights of every color.

The lion said, "The animals that you will now see are guards. A hundred of every kind of animal in the world stand guard along the sides of this cave. No man could ever go through, unless he was with me." Jinook looked, and he saw that they were passing between two rows of elephants, then two rows of giraffes, and then two rows of tigers, then two rows of leopards, and so on. All that day and the next they passed between the guards until Jinook had seen a hundred of every animal there is to be seen in the world, right from the biggest to the smallest. At last they came to the other end of the cave, which opened into a small field completely surrounded by cliffs a mile high. There they spent the night. And Jinook slept curled up close to the lion.

In the morning, when it was light, the lion said, "That tree is the tree of wealth."

Then Jinook saw that standing in the middle of the field was a tree. It looked like an ordinary apple tree, the same as he had often seen before. He was disappointed, for he had expected to see a wonderful tree quite different from any other tree in the world. The lion said, "You can pick a sprig. But tell no one that you have taken it. Hide it in your pocket. And when you get home plant it." Jinook got up to walk to the tree, and he found he was lame no more. So he ran to the tree and climbed up it and picked a sprig. He looked to see if there was any fruit, but there was none. This puzzled him. He went back to the lion and said, "Why do they call it the tree of wealth? I don't see anything on it."

The lion said, "When you get home, plant the sprig in your garden. If you don't say a word about what you've seen since being with me, then you will learn the secret of the tree. Come, we must be going."

Jinook put the sprig in his pocket and climbed on to the lion's back, and away they went back through the cave. In a month they reached the palace again. Then

Jinook was seized with a great longing for his brothers. He said, "All this time my brothers have been suffering. Won't you please free them now?"

"I will," said the lion. "I'll do it for your sake, but not because they deserve it."

So they set out for the ant's house. There the lion gave judgment: Nar was to be allowed to go home. The ants dug him out of the hill, and he was free. When he saw Jinook, he said, "How did you get here? You are lame no more. How did that happen?"

Jinook said, "It is enough that I have come and begged mercy for you. More than that you need not know. If it hadn't been for me, the lion would not have freed you."

Then Nar pretended to be very fond of Jinook. He thanked him and said kind words to him. He acted as if he had always liked Jinook better than any one else in the world. When the lion saw how Nar behaved, he said, "It would be well if you always treated your brother that way. But I'm afraid you are only pretending."

"Oh, no," said Nar. "He is a good brother. I may have treated him badly sometimes. But from now on I shall always treat him well."

"See that you do," said the lion, "for Jinook is worth two of you."

After that they went on to the spider's house, where Sar was freed in the same way. And he, too, made a great fuss about Jinook. The lion said to him, "You seem very fond of your brother. Do you really love him, or are you only pretending?"

"I really do," said Sar. "He is the best brother in the world."

"Be sure to remember those words," said the lion. "Don't forget them as soon as you get home."

"I won't," said Sar. "I'm not that kind."

"I'm not sure whether you are or not," said the lion, looking more as if he doubted than believed Sar's words.

Then they set to talking about how they would get home. Sar thought they should go one way, and Nar thought another. Jinook kept quiet. After Sar and Nar had talked and argued for a while, they turned to the lion and said, "You tell us which is the right way."

"Neither," said the lion. "You'll only get home safely if I send you. And I'll only send you on condition that you promise to be good to Jinook and to ask him no questions about what he has seen here."

"That's easy," said Sar and Nar. "We'll promise you that."

Then the lion roared, and three eagles came lying through the sky and lighted on the ground near the lion. The lion said to them, "Each of you carry one of these boys on your back and take him home. They are brothers and live together."

With these words that the lion spoke, Sar, Nar, and Jinook each climbed on to an eagle's back. The lion shook hands with each of them and said good-bye. Then the eagles flapped their wings and flew off into the sky. In this way the boys got home easily and without having to walk.

The eagles carried them to a forest not far from home. There they left them in a clearing and went away. After the eagles had gone, Sar and Nar said to Jinook, "Tell us why you are lame no more. If you don't tell us, we shall tie you up with vines and leave you here. We want to hear everything. How did you meet the lion? Did he show you the tree?"

Jinook said, "You promised the lion not to ask me. I won't tell you."

"What do we care what we promised the lion," said Sar and Nar. "He is far away and can't harm us. Will you tell us, or won't you?"

"I won't," said Jinook.

"You won't, won't you?" said Sar and Nar. "We'll see whether you will or not." And with these words they seized Jinook, bound him hand and foot, and tied him to a tree. Then they laughed at him and said, "If you'll tell us, we'll let you free. If not, you can stay there for good."

"I won't tell you," said Jinook. "That's all there is to it."

So Sar and Nar left Jinook and went home. When they came to their house, their mother was glad to see them, for she had long thought they would never come back. She asked, "What happened to you? Why have you been away so long? Did you find the tree?"

They told their mother this and that, and she believed they had done wonderful things. They said, "We did what no man has ever done before: we found the tree of wealth. But there was so much gold on it, that we thought it best not to carry it back. We have hidden it where we can find it. We shall go back for it with horses and wagons. Now tell us what you have been doing. Where is Jinook?"

"Didn't he join you?" asked the mother. "He disappeared not long after you left. I thought he might have gone to find you."

"We have not seen him," said Sar and Nar. "He didn't join us."

When the old woman heard these words, she burst into tears, for she had hoped in her heart that all three brothers would come back together. No amount of talking on the part of the boys could stop their mother from crying. She wailed and moaned and made such a fuss, that Sar and Nar were alarmed: they thought she had gone mad. So they hurried out of the house and brought back Jinook. Then the truth came out. The mother punished Sar and Nar, as they deserved to be punished. She kept them in the house day after day and made them work hard all the time. And they were very much ashamed of themselves and begged forgiveness. But their mother had no idea of forgiving them, until she

had punished them as severely as possible. To make
their punishment worse, she gave Jinook whatever he
asked for and let him play as much as he wished. She
said, "You are the best of my boys. I am glad that you
are lame no more. Tell me how you were cured."

"I have promised not to tell," said Jinook.

"Then don't," said the mother. "It is enough for me
to know that you are lame no longer."

As soon as he had a chance, Jinook planted the sprig
in his garden and waited to see what would happen.
Meanwhile Sar and Nar repented and were forgiven.
They became different boys, and they treated Jinook as
brothers should. Time passed, and the tree grew. But
it grew to look just like any other fruit tree. Jinook kept
watching it, expecting to see something wonderful happen. But nothing did. At last, one summer, it was
covered with fruit—beautiful round fruit, blue in color,
with long stems. When Jinook saw it, he thought to
himself, "What can this mean? The fruit is pretty, but
there is no wealth in it. Perhaps it will change into gold
when it ripens." So he looked forward to the day when
the fruit would ripen.

The summer passed and fall came. Then the fruit on
the tree became ripe. But it was still fruit, not gold.
One day Jinook picked one of them off the tree. He
bit it. It was sweet and juicy. So he bit further into
it. Then his teeth struck something hard, which he
thought was a seed. He looked; and, lo and behold, the

fruit was full of seeds, and each seed was a large diamond. In this way he learned the secret of the tree. He picked all the fruit and took all the seeds out, and he had a huge pile of diamonds. Thereafter, every year, he got a big crop of diamonds. He forgave his brothers and shared his fortune with them. His mother had to work no more. And they are all alive and happy to-day.

"IF I'D been Jinook, I'd have kept the diamonds," said Tal. "Sar and Nar didn't deserve to be treated so well."

"Perhaps not," said the old man. "But I guess Jinook knew what was the best thing to do."

"How much do you think all those diamonds were worth?" asked Tal.

"A lot of money," said the old man. "More than you've ever seen."

"That's a great story," said Tal. "I'd like to have been Jinook and seen all those animals. I wonder what it's like to ride on a lion's back? I'd like . . ."

Just then the Wimzies began to come behind the waterfalls. They jumped right through the middle of the falls without hurting themselves at all. They swam across the pool and climbed up the rock to where their houses were. All the while Noom-Zor-Noom watched them. He said, "If you see one with a red head, let me know. That one will be king, and with him we must speak. He alone can be of any help to us."

"There he is now," said Tal. "He just came through the waterfalls. See him over there?"

Noom-Zor-Noom looked; and there was the King of the Wimzies just about to climb to his house. The old man lost no time. He shouted and said, "O king of all the Wimzies, is there anything you wish?"

When the king heard these words, he quickly swam over to where Noom-Zor-Noom was standing. He came out of the water on to the flat rock. Then he turned three somersaults, bowed, and said, "Did you ask me if there was anything I wished?"

Noom-Zor-Noom knew that the Wimzies liked to have their wishes granted better than anything else. So he said, "Anything you wish for, you shall have. But in return you and your people must do something for me."

The king drew himself up to his full six inches of height. And indeed he was a sight to look at with his bluish green body and big, round, red head. He said, "There is one thing I want for myself and my people. I have asked it of many. But none have been able to give it to me. If you will give me that one thing that I want, I will do anything in the world for you."

Noom-Zor-Noom asked, "What is it?"

The king said, "We live in the holes in the rock. All day we swim in the water under the falls. And at night, when we come home, we work changing pebbles into jade beads. We could do our work much easier if we had lights in our houses. But we have no lamps. Now if you will give us each a lamp, we will do what you want us to."

When Noom-Zor-Noom heard this request, he said, "You ask for more than one thing. You ask for many things."

"No, I don't," said the king. "I only ask for one thing—light."

"It's a hard request to grant," said Noom-Zor-Noom. "If I do give you the light you ask for, I shall expect you to do a great deal for me."

"I will," said the king. "We'll do anything you want. Tell me what you have in mind."

Then Noom-Zor-Noom went on and told the king just what he wanted the Wimzies to do. He said, "Not only do I want you to tell me which of the underground rivers goes to Troom. But I want your people to swim up that river and pull our golden basket behind them. It is the only way we have of getting home. Will you do that?"

"That will be easy," said the king. "I thought you were going to ask for something harder than that."

By the time Noom-Zor-Noom had finished talking with the king of the Wimzies, the sun had set and night had come. It was dark under the falls; not much could be seen. Noom-Zor-Noom said to the king, "Call your people, and I will give them each a lamp." Then he turned to Tal and whispered to him, "As soon as the king calls his people, you open the silver box with the pieces of the Milky Way in it, and throw all the pieces into the pool here under the falls." That was all he said, nothing more.

The king of the Wimzies gave a shrill whistle. At once every latch clicked, and all the little golden doors opened. Then Tal threw a handful of the Milky Way into the water. It scattered like a handful of dust, and each little piece shone and sparkled. Before any of the pieces sank to the bottom of the pool, the Wimzies dived in after them. Each Wimzie got a piece, took it back to his house, and kept it there. Each tiny bit made so much light that every Wimzie had a lamp. And they left the doors of their houses open, so that the light came out and lit up everything under the falls.

When the king saw what a wonderful thing had happened, he said, "You have done more than I thought any man could do. You have given each of us a lamp. Now we will take you where you wish to go."

Tal, Noom-Zor-Noom, and Millitinkle got into the golden basket. And the king got in with them. Then all the Wimzies dived into the water and took hold of the basket. They pushed it along to where the three underground rivers came out of the side of the cliff. When they got to that place, the king said, "We want the river that leads to Troom." And as he said it, the letters T-R-O-O-M appeared in glowing green letters over the

mouth of the middle cave. So the Wimzies knew that
that one went to Troom. They swam into the cave, and
followed the river under the cliff. Everything became
pitch black. And all that Tal could hear was the swish-
ing of water against the sides of the cave.

CHAPTER XII

THE VALLEY OF MIRRORS AND THE STORY OF THE COBBLER

ALL THAT NIGHT the Wimzies swam up the underground river with the golden basket. And in the morning they reached the end of the tunnel. When they came out into the light once more, they found themselves in a valley surrounded on all sides by steep mountains. In this valley was the spring where the river began. The Wimzies pulled the basket as far as the spring, and there they stopped. The King of the Wimzies said, "We can't take you beyond this point. Here is the source of the river."

Noom-Zor-Noom said, "You have taken us far enough. We don't wish to go any further. Because of your kindness to us, I am going to give you the golden basket as a present."

"Thank you," said the king. "It will make it easy for us to get back home."

Then Noom-Zor-Noom bade the king good-bye. The king climbed into the basket and ordered all the other Wimzies to do the same. And, when the last Wimzie had scrambled over the edge, the king said, "Give us a push." Noom-Zor-Noom gave the basket a push, and it floated off down the river. And soon all the Wimzies disappeared from sight into the underground passage.

"Now what are we going to do?" asked Tal; for he did not see how they could ever climb out of the valley. "Those mountains are too steep for us to go up."

"They are," said the old man. "No one who has come to this valley has ever been able to make his way out."

"Then why did *we* come?" asked Tal.

"Because it's on the way to Troom," said the old man. "Somehow we must get over those mountains at the other end."

So they set out to walk to the far end of the valley. Before they had gone a great distance from the spring, they came to a dense forest. All the trees were knotted and gnarled, and the leaves were shaped like fans. And so big was each leaf that Tal could almost hide behind it. When he saw them, he said, "I have never seen such big leaves. I didn't know they grew so big."

"Most leaves don't," said Noom-Zor-Noom. "This kind of tree only grows in this valley. The leaves are not soft like most leaves, but they are as hard as wood. And their edges are so sharp that they cut like a knife. For that reason it is dangerous to be in the forest, because if a leaf should fall on you edge-wise, it would cut you badly."

"Do we have to go through the forest?" asked Tal. "I'd hate to be cut by one of those leaves."

"There's only one way of getting through safely," said the old man. "If we wait here until after a wind storm, then most of the leaves that are likely to fall will have been blown off. Then it will be safe to go through."

"What if the wind doesn't blow?" asked Tal.

"We'll have to wait here until it does," said Noom-Zor-Noom. "It would be foolish to start through the forest before we know that the wind has blown."

They sat down by the edge of the forest to wait for the wind to blow. While they sat there, Noom-Zor-Noom read the story of

THE COBBLER

THERE was a cobbler who lived in a village. All his life he had made shoes, but he never made much money. One day he thought, "All these years I have worked hard. Still I am poor. Day after day I do nothing but

N

make shoes for other people. Perhaps if I make a pair for myself, something wonderful will happen."

He set to work and made himself a pair of shoes. He made them well, much better than the ones he made for other people. At last, when they were finished, he put them on; but nothing happened. So he decided to go for a walk. He walked along the side of the sea. A big wave rolled up and swished around his feet. And, lo and behold, the cobbler found that with his new shoes he could walk on the water just as well as he could on the land. He said to himself, "Indeed something wonderful has happened. Now I am better than any other man in the world. I shall be poor no longer. Anything I want, I can have. I shall go to the king. He will be glad to see me. He will pay me well and keep me in his palace. It is not every one that can walk on water the way I can." And he thought what a wonder he really was.

He went back home, closed his shop, and then set out to go to the king. On the way he met some fishermen. They were sad and were sitting on the shore sighing. The cobbler went to them and asked, "What's the matter? Why are you sad?"

The fishermen said, "Our boat has blown away with all our fish. We did not tie it well. We are lost."

"Don't worry," said the cobbler. "I'll get it for you." He walked out on the water and pulled the boat back for the men.

The fishermen said, "Thank you. You are indeed a wonderful man to be able to walk on the water like that. Take half of our fish for the trouble we have caused you. You can sell them and make some money."

The cobbler said, "I am so wonderful I can make all the money I need. I don't want to take yours." And he walked away without taking their fish.

A little farther on he came to a river. Near the river sat a woman. She was crying and was very unhappy. The cobbler went up to her and said, "What's the matter, that you sit here crying?"

The woman said, "I live on the other side of the river. My boat has floated away; and I can't get home. My husband will beat me for not having his supper ready."

"Don't cry," said the cobbler. "I'll carry you across." He picked up the woman and carried her across the river. And on the other side she said to him, "It is wonderful that you can walk on the water like this. No one else in the world can do it. You have been good to me. I can not pay you anything, for I have no money. But come to my house, and I'll give you a beautiful jewel that I have."

"Keep your jewel," said the cobbler. "One jewel would mean nothing to a man who is as wonderful as I am. I shall soon have all the jewels I want." He left the woman without taking her jewel, and he went on his way to the king.

Before he got there, word had already reached the

king about this cobbler who could walk on the water. When he came to the palace, the king greeted him at the door, saying, "You are a wonderful man. I am glad you have come. There are many things I want you to do for me. If you do them, you can have half of my kingdom; and I shall build you a palace of your own."

The cobbler said, "I can do anything in the world. There is nothing I can't do."

He went in with the king and stayed in the palace. The king put him in a room by himself and sent men-servants and maid-servants to wait on him. To hear him talk you would have thought him king himself. He bragged and boasted about what he could do. He talked as if he himself had given his shoes their power, instead of saying it came from he knew not where. And every-thing he said, the king believed.

One day the king said, "I have heard that somewhere across the sea there is a strange land. The mountains are made of pure gold. Whoever can find that land will be richer than any one else in the world. I have not sent ships to it, for I have heard that the coast is guarded by a high wall of water. My ships could not get over such a wall. You go to this land and see if all I have heard is true. If it is, come back here and we'll think of some way to get the gold. You may have half of it." And he told the cobbler just what direction the land lay in and how to get there.

The cobbler said, "That's easy. I'll go."

So the king gave him food and such things as he needed. And the cobbler set off to walk across the sea. Day after day he walked for many days. At last he saw in the distance some mountains of gold. But the land that they rose from was not guarded by any such wall of water as the king had spoken of. The cobbler walked to the land, and there he found a sailor sitting on the shore and near him a pile of gold. He went up to him and said, "I thought this land of gold was protected by a wall of water."

"Only those who have never been here think that," said the sailor. "Who are you, and where do you come from?"

The cobbler said, "I am from such-and-such a place. I am more wonderful than any one else in the world. I can walk on the water."

When the sailor heard how the cobbler bragged, he said, "So can I walk on the water. But I didn't know any one else could. I am just getting ready to start back with all my gold." These words he spoke, but they were not the truth. He was really a shipwrecked sailor who by chance had been blown up on the coast of the land of gold.

The cobbler said, "It's my shoes that give me the power. I made them myself."

The sailor said, "My shoes do the same. Only they also give me the power to fly over the water."

The cobbler, simple soul that he was, believed what

the sailor said. He looked at the man's shoes and saw that they were exactly like his own. He thought to himself, "It would be good if I could change mine for his. Then I could fly over water. It would be more wonderful than walking." But he pretended to think nothing of the sailor's words, and he asked, "Is it true that the mountains here are made of gold?"

"They are," said the sailor. "Look at all I have dug. But you must go far back in the land. There is no gold near the coast."

All that day the cobbler stayed with the sailor. He asked him many questions about how to get to the mountains of gold. And the sailor told him all he knew. When night came, they lay down on the sand to sleep. In the middle of the night the cobbler got up. With great care he exchanged his own shoes for those of the sailor. After he had laced the sailor's shoes on his own feet, he thought how clever he was and went to sleep.

In the morning the sailor looked at his feet, and he knew at once what had happened. He said nothing. He put all his gold into a sack, got up, and said, "I must leave you now. Here are my pick and shovel. You will have no trouble finding gold. It is all around here." Then he bade the cobbler good-bye and walked out to sea.

The cobbler never thought of trying the shoes. He hurried to the mountains and dug for gold. The more he dug, the more he wanted. So he stayed there digging and never once thought of going back to the king. All he thought of was how he could get the gold for himself without having to share it with the king. A year passed. Still he stayed there digging gold.

In the meantime the king wondered what had happened to the cobbler. He waited and waited: the cobbler did not come back. He said to himself, "Can something have happened? He may have fallen into the sea and drowned. I had better take a ship and go look for him." He ordered a ship made ready, and he and his men set out to find the cobbler. They sailed across the sea until they came to the land of gold. And when the king saw that there was no wall of water at all, he was ashamed of himself for having sent the cobbler. They sailed close to the shore, and they found the cobbler standing by a pile of gold so high that it looked like a hill. The king called to him and said, "We have come to get you and your gold. You have done well."

"I have," said the cobbler. "I have dug all the gold I could."

The king and his men landed. They loaded the ship with gold and set sail for home. And they took the cobbler with them. All the time he was planning how he could get away from the king. He wanted to buy some ships for himself and go back for more gold. He did not want to share it with the king. He thought, "Why should I who am so wonderful share it with him? I went and found it. It all belongs to me." And he never thought that but for the king he would not have known about the gold. As they sailed along, suddenly the wind dropped: it became calm. For many days the ship did not move. The cobbler went to the king and said, "We cannot stay here like this. Our ship has too much of a load. Give me a bag of gold. I'll fly back home and get another ship to come and take some of our load." But what he meant to do was to go away and not come back. He wanted the sack of gold to buy himself a ship.

The king said, "You can walk on the water. But you cannot fly."

The cobbler said, "I have learned to fly too. There is nothing these shoes can't do. They will carry me through the air like a bird."

The king said, "You are more wonderful than I thought. Take as much gold as you want and go. You will save our lives."

So the cobbler took a sack and filled it with gold. Then he said to the king, "You watch! Then you'll see what wonderful shoes I really made. You have seen only half of what they do. I'll run and jump off the side of the boat. I'll fly away without touching the water."

The king said, "Hurry back for us with another ship."

The cobbler really believed he would be able to fly. He took his sack of gold and ran across the ship. Then he gave a jump and shot far out over the water. But instead of flying, he fell into the sea. He went down to the bottom and came up without his sack of gold. He shouted, "Help, I am drowning!"

The king said, "I thought you could fly."

The cobbler shouted, "Save me, and I'll give you anything you want." So the king threw a rope over and pulled the cobbler back on board. And he was so terrified that he told the king about the sailor. When the king heard how the cobbler had stolen the sailor's shoes, he would not believe another word the man said. Then the cobbler's whole plan came to light. The king made him a prisoner. He took him back and told every one what he had tried to do. And everybody laughed at the cobbler and asked him about the shoes, which he did not have.

AS NOOM-ZOR-NOOM read the last word of the story, the wind began to blow. Harder and harder it blew, until the leaves rattled and scraped against each other with so much noise that Tal could not make his own voice heard. Noom-Zor-Noom pulled him back and made him stand at a safe distance from the forest. Then, when the wind had died down, the old man said, "If we hurry, we can get through now. We needn't worry about any leaves falling on us: they have all fallen."

They hurried forward and ran through the forest as fast as they could. At the other side they came to a flat open space that extended for miles ahead of them. This open space was dotted with what seemed to be thousands of small, round pools about twenty feet across. They were just far enough apart so that a man might make his way between them. There were no ripples on them: they were as smooth as glass.

Tal said, "What are these pools? The whole place is full of them."

"They aren't pools," said Noom-Zor-Noom. "Each one is a mirror. See the way they reflect the light."

"Yes," said Tal. "But what are they for?"

"To look into," said Millitinkle, flapping her ears and making the little bells tinkle. "That's what a mirror is always for. So, you see, your question was quite unnecessary."

"I suppose it was," said Tal. "But who looks into them?"

"That's a real question," said the donkey, thoughtfully. "I'll have to think about that." Then she turned to the old man and asked, "Will it be all right if I tell him?"

"If he'll promise not to tell any one else," said Noom-Zor-Noom.

"Will you promise?" asked Millitinkle.

"Of course I will," said Tal.

". . . will promise what?" asked the donkey.

"Not to tell," said Tal.

Then Millitinkle became solemn, as if she were going to tell something very serious. She looked down for a moment and pawed the ground with her hoof. Then she said, "This is the most secret place in all the world. No man has ever come here and gone back to tell about it; for those who come have never been able to find their way out. To cross this valley, you have to follow the paths between the mirrors. But there is only one path that leads across. All the others lead to the dens of terrible monsters." Then the donkey stopped, as if that was all she had to say.

"But I don't see anything so wonderful in that," said Tal.

"I knew that's what you'd say," answered Millitinkle. "That's why I stopped when I did."

"Aren't you going to tell me any more?" asked Tal.

"Yes," said the donkey. "But first you must promise me again that you won't tell."

Then Tal promised again. After that, the donkey went on and told him about the Valley of Mirrors. She said, "Every moonlight night this valley is filled with people. Fairies, gnomes, witches, djinns, and all such people, come here from all over the world."

"What do they come for?" asked Tal.

"Each of them has a mirror. And each comes to that mirror on moonlight nights to comb his hair," said the donkey. "This valley is where they always come to do that. If you happened to be here on such a night, you would see them all. They sit and comb their hair and chat about the wonderful things they have seen and done."

"I'd like to see them," said Tal. "Let's spend the night here."

"We can't," said Noom-Zor-Noom. "If they saw us, they would keep us here forever."

"I wouldn't like that," said Tal. "But how are we going to get out? I should think the easiest thing to do would be to walk across the mirrors."

"You can't do that," said the old man. "They spin under your feet."

When Tal heard this, all he wanted to do was to step on one of the mirrors. He said, "I'm going to try it." And with these words he ran over and stepped on to one of the mirrors. When he tried to walk, the mirror turned under his feet. And before he knew it, he was running to try to keep up with the mirror. The next minute he was thrown off the mirror and fell in a heap on the ground. He picked himself up and said, "I'm not going to try that again."

"I guess not," said the donkey with a loud laugh. Then she burst out laughing again, and she laughed so hard that she had to sit down. The tears streamed out of her eyes, and she shook all over, just like jelly.

"What are you laughing at?" asked Tal.

"At you," said Millitinkle. "That's the funniest thing I ever saw."

"You wouldn't think it was so funny if it had happened to you," said Tal. "*I* don't think it's funny."

"Of course you don't. But I do," said the donkey, and she doubled up with laughter again.

Then Tal got laughing at Millitinkle, because she looked so funny. He had never seen a donkey laugh so hard before, and the faces she made were sights to see. And there the two of them would have stayed all day laughing at one another, had not Noom-Zor-Noom made them stop. He said, "Stop! We've got to do something about getting out of this valley. It's no time to be laughing." When the donkey saw that her master meant what he said, she pulled herself together, but not without making a lot of gurgling, gasping sounds that gave Tal the giggles all over again. But, at last, they both stopped. Then the old man turned to Tal and said, "You can now see that we wouldn't get far if we started across the mirrors."

"How are we going to get out of here, then?" asked Tal, becoming quite serious. "Do you know the way?"

"We are going to stay here until the sun is not so hot," said the old man. "Then I'll show you what to do."

In the evening, after the sun had gone down behind the mountains, Tal and Noom-Zor-Noom gathered some leaves. They carried them to the edge of the nearest mirror, and there they set them down in a pile. Noom-Zor-Noom said, "The first thing to do is to stick these leaves around the edge of this mirror." And then he went over and broke a branch off one of the trees. When he had broken it off, the sap ran out and dripped on to the ground. It was just like glue: it could be used to stick things together so hard that they never came apart. He dipped the ends of the leaves into the sap; and one by one he stuck them on the mirror, until the whole edge was surrounded by a circle of fans. Then he bent each of the leaves up a little, so that one side was higher than the other. After all this was done, and the sap had dried, he said to Millitinkle, "You alone can get us out of this valley. Without you, we are lost."

Millitinkle flapped her ears; the little golden bells tinkled; and she said, "Tell me what to do, and I'll do it."

Noom-Zor-Noom said, "You are to step on the mirror and lie down on your side, so that we can reach your feet from the edge."

Millitinkle did as she was told. Tal and Noom-Zor-Noom held on to the leaves to keep the mirror from turning, while the donkey stepped on and lay down. Then Noom-Zor-Noom took a stick and daubed her hooves with sap, just enough to keep her from slipping but not enough to glue her down. After that she got up. Noom-Zor-Noom put the crystal block on her back and said to Tal, "Climb on top of the block." Tal did; and the old man climbed up after him. There they sat and held on for all they were worth. Noom-Zor-Noom told Millitinkle to run at full speed. As she ran, the mirror turned under her feet; but the sap kept her from slipping off. Finally she made the mirror turn so fast that the force of the wind on the fan-shaped leaves lifted the whole thing into the air. The faster the donkey ran, the higher up they went. In this way they sailed out of the valley and soared over the mountains at the far end.

CHAPTER XIII

THE HOME OF LIGHTNING AND THE SILVER ROAD TO TROOM

DURING THE NIGHT, while they were still in the sky, a great storm came up. Black clouds appeared, thunder rumbled, and lightning flashed. The mirror was blown this way and that way like a leaf. It made no difference what Millitinkle did, the mirror would not come down: it stayed up in the sky. All of a sudden a whirlwind caught it. Round and round it spun, faster and faster than it had ever spun before. So fast did it go that Tal could hold on no longer. He slipped off the crystal block, and as he slipped he caught hold of Noom-Zor-Noom's leg. This pulled the old man off. And the two of them went flying through the sky with nothing to hold on to but each other. They left Millitinkle alone on the mirror. She did not fall off because of the sap on her feet.

Before Tal and Noom-Zor-Noom had dropped far, a streak of lightning came rushing through the sky. It coiled itself around them and carried them off to the top of a high mountain. It took them into a cave, and there it dropped them. And, the next thing that happened, the lightning turned into a beautiful girl with long golden hair that reached down to her feet. She said, "I saw you falling through the sky. So I picked you up and brought you here."

When Tal and Noom-Zor-Noom saw the girl, they trembled with fright. They did not know whether she meant to do them harm or good. The old man said, "It is wonderful what has happened to us. A streak of lightning saved our lives. Who are you, and where did you come from?"

"I am a streak of lightning," said the girl. "Watch! and you will see." With these words, she wrapped her golden hair around her until every inch of her body was covered. And before Tal and Noom-Zor-Noom knew what was happening, she turned into a streak of lightning that flashed and danced about the cave. In another minute she turned back into a girl again.

Noom-Zor-Noom said, "I have never seen any one like you before. Maybe you can tell me where we are?"

"This cave is the home of lightning," said the girl. "My sisters and I live here with our father. I have ninety-nine sisters. Each of us has golden hair, and each of us can turn into a streak of lightning. We would rather be lightning than anything else in the world. But our father does not like to have us change. So he keeps us shut up in this cave. Every now and then we break loose and run and dance through the sky. This makes him angry. He puts on his winged shoes and chases us. And his voice is terrible to hear when he scolds and grumbles and shouts. He drives us out of the sky and back to the cave again. And here we stay until we can find some way of breaking loose."

"I think I've heard his voice," said Tal. "Does it sound like thunder?"

"His voice is thunder," said the girl. "Hear him? He is coming now."

As she spoke, a streak of lightning came into the cave and turned into a girl with golden hair. Then came another and another and another, until all the hundred sisters were in the cave. After that there was a great deal of grumbling and scolding at the mouth of the cave. Finally an iron door was slammed shut and bolted. For a moment all was dark. Then the cave lit up with a mysterious blue light. And one by one the girls came up and spoke to Tal and Noom-Zor-Noom.

The old man told them his story, how he had lost his donkey and his crystal block. And he was sad, for he did not think he would ever find Millitinkle again, to say nothing of getting to Troom. The girls heard all he had to say and were sorry for him. One of them said, "We shall do everything we can for you. But we must all stay here until we find some way of breaking loose. Our father is angry. He will not even come to see us. All he will do for us is sit outside the door and watch, so that none of us can break loose."

Noom-Zor-Noom asked, "Is there no way of getting out that you know of?"

"None," said the girls, "unless our father feels sorry for us and opens the door. When it is locked from the outside, we have no way of opening it."

So Tal and Noom-Zor-Noom stayed with the hundred sisters. And every day that passed brought the time nearer when the old man should be in Troom. Tal heard no more stories. And Noom-Zor-Noom began to give up any hope of ever getting away.

One day Tal came to him and said, "I think I know how to get out."

"How?" said Noom-Zor-Noom. "Tell me what you think."

"Tal said, "I have golden hair just like the hundred sisters. Only mine is short and theirs is long. Some night let me go to the door of the cave and say, 'Father, I have made up my mind to dance through the sky no more. I have cut off all my hair. Open the door and you can feel my head.' He will be so pleased with these words, that he will open the door to feel my hair. When he does this, the sisters can break loose and carry us with them."

Noom-Zor-Noom said, "That is a good plan. Let us tell it to the sisters."

So they told their plan to the girls. And the girls were sure that it could be carried out. But one of them said, "We can take you through the air. But how are we going to get you to earth?" Then they talked among themselves and decided that if each one cut off a little of her

would be enough to make a parachute. So
, and they wove the hair into a parachute.
And the girl that was to carry Tal and Noom-Zor-Noom
folded up the parachute and put it under her arm. Then
they all made ready to go.

In the middle of the night Tal went to the door and
knocked on it. A gruff voice asked, "Who are you and
what do you want?"

Tal said, "I am one of your daughters. All my life I
have caused you trouble. Now I am sorry. I have made
up my mind never to turn into lightning again. Let me
out, that I may show you what I have done. All the
others have done the same."

The voice said, "You have fooled me many times before. How do I know that you will not fool me this
time?"

Tal said, "I have cut all my hair off. More than that I
cannot do. I can never be a streak of lightning again.
Open the door a little and you can feel my head."

The father, when he heard these words, believed that
his daughter spoke the truth. He was pleased to think
that she should have done such a thing, for without her
hair it was impossible for her to change into lightning.
So he unbolted the door and opened it a little. Then he
reached in with his hand and felt Tal's hair. He said,
"You have done what I never thought you would do.
Put your head out so that I may see it." He opened the
door a bit wider, and Tal stuck out the top of his head.

It was so dark that the father could only see the golden color of the hair. So he had no reason to believe that it was not one of his daughters at the door. He said, "You may come out." He opened the door. And with that the hundred sisters turned into lightning and flashed by their father, blinding him with their light. Before he could even shut the door, they had all escaped; even the one with the parachute, who coiled herself around Tal and Noom-Zor-Noom and carried them away. The father, when he saw them all go, shouted, and scolded and grumbled. And he made such a noise that it sounded as if the sky itself were tumbling down.

All of the streaks of lightning danced through the sky until they were over the plateau on which was Troom. There the one that had the parachute opened it, while another one held on to Tal and Noom-Zor-Noom. Then they tied the old man and the boy to the parachute and dropped them. After that all the lightning hurried away and went to another part of the sky.

Tal and Noom-Zor-Noom did not fall straight down: a wind was blowing, and it carried them a long way off. They came to earth on the side of a mountain. As soon as their feet touched the ground, the golden parachute disappeared into thin air: they could not see it anywhere. Noom-Zor-Noom said, "We must spend the night here. It is too dark for us to find our way."

"Where do you think we are?" asked Tal. "And what do you think has happened to Millitinkle?"

"I don't know," said Noom-Zor-Noom with a sigh. "We could not be much worse off than we are. I have lost my donkey. I have lost my stories. And I have lost all track of the time. It seems to me that a great many days have passed since we fell off the mirror. For all I know the story-tellers may have told their stories by this time. If so, it will make little difference whether or not I find the crystal block again. But I do hope that Milli-tinkle is not lost for good. I don't know what I'd do without her." He sighed again and was so sad that Tal became alarmed.

"Everything will turn out all right," said Tal. "I know it will. We'll find everything, and we'll get to Troom in time."

"It's easy to say that," said Noom-Zor-Noom. "Even if we do find everything, there will be no time to read you all the stories. The reason that I brought you with me was that you might hear them all and choose the one you liked best."

"Any of the ones that I've heard so far are good enough to open the Door," said Tal. "Don't worry. Things will turn out all right."

But nothing that the boy said cheered Noom-Zor-Noom. He grew sadder and sadder and sadder. And all that night they sat on the mountainside waiting for dawn to come. They did not sleep a wink, so anxious were they to find out where they were and how far they still had to travel.

HE OPENED THE DOOR AND THE HUNDRED SISTERS TURNED INTO LIGHTNING
AND FLASHED BY THEIR FATHER.

With the first light of morning Noom-Zor-Noom looked about and said, "We are nearer to Troom than I thought. That trail is the one we want to follow." He pointed to a trail that ran up the side of the mountain not far from where they stood. "All we can do is hurry along and hope for the best."

So they set out. They followed the trail as far as it went. It led them up the mountain and over the top. After that they went up another mountain and over the top of that one. Then they came to a row of mountains that seemed to form a wall, so close together were they and so high. Up this the trail went. They followed it, and late in the afternoon they found themselves near a pass. Noom-Zor-Noom said to Tal, "Soon we shall come to Beego the Blacksmith's. He will know what day it is, and he may know something about Millitinkle. For he lives on the border of the plateau on which is Troom." Then they started to cross over.

This pass, at the point where it crossed the highest part of the mountain wall, went through a deep cut in the rocks. On either side cliffs rose for five hundred feet or more. Through this cut Tal and Noom-Zor-Noom walked. At the end they came to a house that was built right across the cut between the cliffs. There the trail ended; it went no further.

Noom Zor-Noom said, "That house ahead of us belongs to Beego the Blacksmith. No one can follow the trail any further without going through his house."

Tal said, "I shouldn't think he'd like to have people going through all the time. Doesn't it bother him?"

"Not enough people come to bother him," said Noom-Zor-Noom. "There are not many that get this far on the road to Troom. The few that do, Beego is always glad to see."

Noom-Zor-Noom walked up and knocked at the door, which was big, just as big as the doors most smithies have. The door opened, and Beego came out. He was a huge man, almost a giant. He had silver hair and a silver mustache, and his clothes were all made of silver too. In his hand he carried a silver hammer. He looked at Noom-Zor-Noom and said, "I thought you must be coming soon. Your donkey has been here with me for some time. What happened to you?"

"Is Millitinkle really here?" asked Noom-Zor-Noom. And his eyes filled with tears, so glad was he to know that she was safe. "Where is she?"

"Right in here," said Beego, opening the door wider.

Tal and Noom-Zor-Noom went into the blacksmith's shop, and there was Millitinkle with the crystal block still on her back. When she saw her master, she flapped her ears and made the little bells tinkle loudly. Then she said, "What happened to you? Why did you fall off? I stayed on the mirror and landed not far from here."

"We couldn't hold on any longer," said Noom-Zor-Noom. "We slipped off. A streak of lightning saved us and carried us to its home. There wonderful things happened." He went on and told the donkey all about where they had been and what they had seen. Then Millitinkle told her story. And the three of them were glad to be together once more.

All this time Beego stood by and listened. When they had finished, the blacksmith said, "If you hope to reach Troom in time to tell your story, you must go soon. To-morrow night King Tazzarin will hear the stories."

Noom-Zor-Noom asked, "Have any of the other story-tellers left Troom?"

"No," said Beego. "You are the only one who has gone to the outside world. And I was afraid that you would not get back in time."

"So was I," said Noom-Zor-Noom.

After that Noom-Zor Noom and Beego talked of many things. And while they were talking, Tal looked about the shop. He saw that everything in it was made of silver. The anvil was silver, the tools were silver, and all the horse-shoes were silver. He thought, "This man must be rich to have all his things made of silver. I'd like to have some of them myself." He could not take his eyes off what he saw, and he had to look at each thing by itself. So he went around the shop and saw all there was to see. When he had seen everything, he ran up to Noom-Zor-Noom and said, "I like this place. I'd like to stay here for a while. I could watch Beego work, and you could tell me stories."

Noom-Zor-Noom said, "That would be nice! But we haven't the time. You heard Beego say that if I am going to read my story before King Tazzarin, I must be in Troom to-morrow night. We can't stay here. We must be off this minute."

"We can't go until we get our silver shoes," said Millitinkle. "Without them we can't walk on the road."

"Of course not," said Noom-Zor-Noom. "You have yours put on first. Tal and I will wait until you are through."

"Why do we have to have silver shoes?" asked Tal. "I don't want to have shoes put on by a blacksmith. Only animals do that. Men go to cobblers."

"You have to have silver shoes to walk on the silver road to Troom," said Noom-Zor-Noom. "And Beego has to put them on for you. No one else can do it."

Beego set to work and put silver shoes on all four of the donkey's feet. Then he put silver soles on Noom-Zor-Noom's shoes. And when he was through with them, he said to Tal, "Step up here, and I'll shoe you."

"I don't want to be shod," said Tal.

"You have to be shod before you can leave me," said Beego.

So Tal stepped up to the anvil. And while he stood there Beego made him the most wonderful pair of silver sandals. He made them so fast and so skillfully that Tal could hardly follow him with his eyes. He fastened them to the boy's feet with silver bands. Then he said,

"Now you may go. When you come back this way, you must leave the shoes with me."

"Mayn't I keep them?" asked Tal; for now that he had the sandals he did not want to give them up.

"That depends on whether or not you come back," said Beego. "If you come back you will have to leave them here."

"He'll be back, and he'll leave the sandals here," said Noom-Zor-Noom. "He's just making a visit, that's all."

Beego said, "Now you can go on to Troom if you wish. But before you go, let me ask you one question: What are you going to do with this boy? You know that King Tazzarin will let no children come into Troom. You can take Tal to the walls of the city. But beyond there he cannot go. Wouldn't you like to leave him here with me?"

"That depends on him," said Noom-Zor-Noom. "If he wants to go as far as the city, he can. If not, he can stay here with you. Which do you want to do, Tal?"

"I want to go on with you," said Tal. "I want to see what Troom looks like. I won't mind waiting outside the walls."

"But what if I don't open the Golden Door and am thrown into prison?" said the old man. "Then what will happen to you?"

"I can come back here," said Tal. "That would be easy. But please don't leave me here. I want to go with you to Troom."

"You take him with you," said Beego. "If I hear that you don't open the Door, then I'll come after Tal and bring him back here. He can live with me."

"Yes, we can do that," said Tal. "I'd love to live here with Beego, if anything happens to you."

Thereupon, they made up their minds that Tal was to go on to Troom with Noom-Zor-Noom. Beego led them to the farthest end of his shop, where there was another door. He unlatched the door and threw it open. When Tal looked out, he saw a great plain stretching before him as far as his eyes could see. It was perfectly flat, and there were no trees or bushes of any kind growing on it. Starting at the door and going straight across the plain was a road all made of pure silver. It was wide enough for two wagons to pass; and it seemed to have just been polished, so bright and shiny was it.

"Is that our road?" asked Tal, pointing to the silver highway. For he did not dare step on it, it looked so clean and new.

"That's it," said Noom-Zor-Noom.

Then, one by one, they thanked Beego for what he had done, and said good-bye to him. After that they went out through the door and were off on the silver road to Troom.

CHAPTER XIV

TROOM

ALL THAT DAY and all that night they followed the silver road across the plain. They saw nothing; no men, no animals, no living thing of any kind. Not once did they stop, not even to sleep or eat. But Tal did not grow tired, for his silver sandals carried him along with no effort whatsoever. On the morning of the second day they came to an amber cliff, so high that when Tal stood at the bottom and looked up, the top was out of sight. At the foot of this cliff the road ended; and where the road ended, there was a door. Noom-Zor-Noom stopped and said, "No one can get to the top of this cliff without first becoming part animal."

"What do you mean?" asked Tal.

"I'll show you," said Noom-Zor-Noom. He opened the door, and the three of them went into a square room. The walls of the room were covered with shelves, and on the shelves were rows and rows of miniature animals carved out of amber. There was an amber elephant, an amber tiger, an amber eagle, an amber kangaroo, an amber giraffe, and as many other kinds of animals as you can think of. In front of each animal was a little amber cup filled with a clear liquid that looked very much like

water. Noom-Zor-Noom picked up one of the cups and said, "This cup was in front of the elephant. If I take a sip of the liquid, then I'll become part elephant."

"What part?" asked Tal.

"My nose will grow into a trunk," said Noom-Zor-Noom.

"But that won't help you get up the cliff," said Tal. "I don't see what's the use of drinking it."

"There's none," said Noom-Zor-Noom. "But if I drank from the cup in front of the eagle, then I would have wings and could fly to the top of the cliff."

"I see what you mean," said Tal. "I could drink from the cup in front of the crow, and I'd grow black wings and could fly. But if I drank from the cup in front of the dog, I'd only learn how to bark. Is that right?"

"Yes," said Noom-Zor-Noom. "But there's no way of telling just what part of you will change. And, as you can only drink from one cup, it's important that you

choose some animal that will be likely to help you get up
the cliff. Otherwise, you'll have to stay at the bottom."

"I'm going to drink from the same one you do," said
Tal. "Then I'll know what's going to happen to me."

"You can't do that," said Noom-Zor-Noom. "We
each have to take a different cup. And you must swallow only one sip. If you take more than that, there's no
telling what will happen to you."

"What does Millitinkle do?" asked Tal.

"She has to drink too," said Noom-Zor-Noom. "She
can't get up without changing."

After that they went around the room and looked at
all the little animals one by one. Then Millitinkle said,
"If I had hind legs like those of a kangaroo, in one hop I
could reach the top of the cliff." With these words, she
picked up the cup in front of the kangaroo and took a
sip of the liquid. By the time she had put the cup back
in place and walked through the door, her legs began to
grow. In a few minutes she had such tremendous kangaroo legs, that she could hop hundreds of yards at a
time. She turned to Noom-Zor-Noom and said, "I'm
going now. I'll see you at the top of the cliff." And off
she went down the silver road . . . hop . . . hop . . .
HOP!! Soon she was a mere speck miles away across
the plain. Before she had disappeared altogether, she
turned around and started back at full speed. Faster and
faster she came, and closer and closer, until it seemed
that in one more hop she would dash herself headlong

against the cliff. But she never took that last hop. Instead, she gave a terrific jump and shot up into the air. Up and up she went, straight over Tal's head, and out of sight. And as she did not come down again, Noom-Zor-Noom knew that she must have reached the top.

"Will I be able to do that too?" asked Tal. "It must be fun to hop along like that."

"You'll have to do something else," said the old man. "No one else can drink out of the kangaroo's cup to-day."

"Tell me what cup to drink out of," said Tal. "I'll drink out of any one you say."

"I can't do that," said the old man. "You'll have to choose for yourself. Anyhow, I'm going next, so that you'll be able to watch me and know what to do."

"I don't want to be left alone," said Tal. "Let me go along with you."

"That's not possible," said Noom-Zor-Noom. "I've got to be at the top to look out for you when you come. There's nothing to be afraid of. Choose your animal and drink out of the cup in front of it. Then do what you feel like doing."

"I might choose the wrong one. Then I'd be left here," said Tal. "And I'd never see you again."

"Don't worry about that," said the old man. "If you want to be absolutely safe, drink from the cup in front of any one of the birds. That's what I am going to do."

Then Noom-Zor-Noom drank from the cup in front of the eagle. After that, he went out of the room and stood near the foot of the cliff. While he stood there, his arms slowly grew feathery and turned into wings. He flapped them and said, "I'm going now. When you've had your drink, come out of the room and shut the door." With these words he spread his wings and flew off to the top of the cliff.

Tal watched him disappear from sight, then he went inside the room. He thought, "Which cup had I better try? I have seen what the kangaroo does, and I have seen Noom-Zor-Noom grow wings like an eagle. It would be fun if I tried something else." He forgot all about what the old man had told him: that he would be safe if he took a cup from in front of a bird. Instead he went from animal to animal, wondering which one to try. When he came to the giraffe, he stopped and said, "If I drank from your cup, I would grow long legs and could step to the top of the cliff. That would be more fun than anything else." He reached up and took the cup in his hand. He put it to his lips and sipped the liquid. It tasted so good, that without another thought he drank the whole cup dry. Then he hurried from the room and slammed the door behind him. All of a sudden his legs and his neck began to grow, but his body stayed the same. Soon he was so unsteady on his feet that he had to lean back against the cliff to balance himself. Still his neck and legs kept on growing. His head got farther and farther away from his body, and his body got farther and farther away from the ground. He looked down, and he could see his sandals shining like two silver specks far below. "Am I never going to stop?" he thought. "No giraffe ever had a neck or legs like this. Perhaps I should not have drunk so much." Meanwhile he went right on growing until his head was at the top of the cliff, his body half way up, and his feet on the ground. Then he turned around and saw Millitinkle and Noom-Zor-Noom. He said, "I drank from the cup in front of the giraffe. Look at what has happened to me. What shall I do?"

"How much did you drink?" asked Noom-Zor-Noom.

"All," said Tal.

"I told you to take only a sip," said the old man. "I can't do anything for you now. When your body comes by, if I can pull you back and make you sit down here, then you will become your own size again."

"I don't want to grow any more," shouted Tal, for all the time his neck was getting longer and his head farther away from the top of the cliff. "Please stop me. I'll never disobey you again. I promise you I won't. Please! Please! . . . Please!"

"I've got to wait until your body comes by," shouted Noom-Zor-Noom. "When your legs are so long that your body is up here, then I'll try to make you sit down. If once you sit on the edge of the cliff, you will shrink to your own size again."

"What did you say?" shouted Tal. "Say it again. I didn't hear you."

"I said . . ." started Noom-Zor-Noom; then he stopped, for he saw that Tal's head was too high up in the sky for the boy to hear anything. So he and Millitinkle sat down and waited. They waited for a long time; and finally a pair of shoulders appeared, then a back, and then a pair of hips. "Come on," said Noom-Zor-Noom to the donkey, "take hold of his sarong and pull with all your might." Millitinkle took hold of Tal's sarong with her teeth, and the old man pulled on it with his hands. In this way, with a great deal of effort, they managed to make Tal sit back on to the edge of the cliff. Then his legs began to shrink up, and his head shrunk down, until he became his own size once more. He turned to the old man and said, "Is this the top of the cliff? Did my legs grow that long?"

"They did," said Noom-Zor-Noom. "No one ever came up the cliff that way before. It's lucky you didn't go on growing forever."

"I'm glad I didn't," said Tal. "I don't ever want to grow that tall again."

"You shouldn't have drunk so much," said the old man, severely. "I told you to take only a sip."

"I know it," said Tal. "I'm sorry I did what you told me not to do. But it was so good I couldn't stop drinking. I didn't know what it was going to do to me."

"You know now," said Noom-Zor-Noom. "The next time, perhaps you'll do what I tell you."

"I will," said Tal. "I promise you I will. Won't you tell me what made me stop growing?"

Noom-Zor-Noom said, "The minute you sat down on the top of the cliff, it broke the spell."

"What spell?" asked Tal.

"The spell that the liquid cast over you, when you drank it," said Noom-Zor-Noom. "The same thing happened to Millitinkle and to me. Otherwise we'd still be part animal. It would be unfortunate to have to stay part animal all your life. But that's what happens to those who drink the liquid and are not able to get up the amber cliff."

"I'm glad I got up," said Tal. "But why did we have to come? Where are we now?"

"We're on the plateau that Troom is on. All we have to do is follow the silver road and we'll go straight to Troom."

"But where's the road?" asked Tal. "I haven't seen it."

"It's right behind you," said the old man.

Tal turned around, and there was the silver road not far from where he sat. He said, "I thought it stopped at the bottom of the cliff."

"It did," said Noom-Zor-Noom. "But it begins again up here. If we start walking right now, we'll be in Troom this evening."

"Aren't you going to read me any more stories?" asked Tal.

"I'm afraid there's not time," said the old man with a sigh. "I may have a chance later to read one more, but that will be all. You be thinking them over, so you can tell me which you like best. I'll ask you, when we get near Troom. Now we must be hurrying along."

The three of them got up and started off on the silver road. All the rest of that day they followed it across the plateau. Late in the afternoon Tal saw in the distance a flat-topped hill that was all white and rose high above the surrounding land. He looked at it and said, "What's that white hill in the distance? It looks to me as if it were covered with snow."

"That's the hill that Troom is on," said the old man. "It's not covered with snow. It's all made of ivory. The city of Troom is built on top of it."

"Why don't we see any houses?" asked Tal.

"Because there's a high ivory wall around the city," said Noom-Zor-Noom. "The wall is higher than the tops of the houses. That's why you can't see them."

"What do the houses look like?" asked Tal.

"They're shaped like eggs standing on end," said Noom-Zor-Noom. "And they're all painted bright colors."

"Like Easter-eggs?" asked Tal.

"Exactly," said the old man.

"It must be fun to live in houses like that," said Tal. "You must make King Tazzarin let me into the city, so I can see the houses. He will, won't he?"

Noom-Zor-Noom said nothing; he walked on, as if he had not heard the boy's words. The road led them straight toward the hill, until they were quite near.

Then it turned, circled completely around the hill seven times, and ended up at the foot of a flight of silver stairs. There Noom-Zor-Noom stopped and sat down on the bottom step. He said, "This is as far as you can come with me. No children are allowed to go beyond here. Sit down while I read you one more story. I think there's time for it before the sun goes down. Then you can wait here till I come back. If I don't come back, Beego the Blacksmith knows where you are. He'll take you to his house."

"Please don't leave me," said Tal. "I want to go into the city."

"You can't," said Noom-Zor-Noom. "If you come in with me, King Tazzarin will seize you and put you to death."

"I don't care," said Tal. "I'm not going to let you go without me."

Noom-Zor-Noom shook his head and said, "You mustn't act that way. There's nothing I'd rather do than take you. But it can't be done. You sit down and listen to this story. Then tell me which one you like best of all those you've heard."

"I don't want to," said Tal. "I want to go to Troom."

"You've got to tell me," said Noom-Zor-Noom. "The only reason I brought you along was because I thought you could choose a story that would open the Door."

"I know it," said Tal. "I'm sorry I spoke like that. You read the story, and I'll listen."

Then Noom-Zor-Noom began to read a story called
THE GREAT GIANT BUNGGAH. But before he
got halfway through it, the sun set; and there was not
enough light to read by. He said, "I can't see to read
any more. I'll have to leave the story unfinished."

"Read just a little more," said Tal. "It's the best story
you've read yet."

"It's too dark to see," said the old man. "But I'll tell
you how the rest of the story goes." And he went on and
told Tal as much of the story as he could remember.
Then he said, "If you wish, I can tell you how some of
the other stories go that I haven't read. Perhaps you'd
like them better."

"You don't have to," said Tal. "I know that the story
about the giant will open the Door. Any child would
like that story."

"Are you sure?" asked Noom-Zor-Noom.

"I know it will," said Tal.

Then Noom-Zor-Noom was pleased. He believed
that the story Tal chose would really open the Door. He
said, "If you like the story as much as that, I shall read
it before the king. I didn't think any of my stories would
please you so much."

"That one does," said Tal. "It's the best story I've
ever heard. But I may be wrong."

"You can't be," said Noom-Zor-Noom. "I have a feeling that your choice is right. All along I've known that
you would save me from prison."

"I haven't saved you yet," said Tal, for he was afraid

that Noom-Zor-Noom was too hopeful. "I don't want you to be disappointed."

Then Millitinkle flapped her ears; the little golden bells tinkled; and she said, "Tal has chosen the right story. It will open the Door."

When Noom-Zor-Noom heard these words that his donkey spoke, he had no more doubts. He said, "Millitinkle always speaks the truth. So she must be right this time."

"Of course I'm right," said Millitinkle. "But you should do something for Tal, because he has chosen the right story."

"What can I do, more than I've done?" asked the old man.

"You can take him to Troom," said Millitinkle.

"How can I?" asked Noom-Zor-Noom. "You know King Tazzarin's orders."

"Let Tal crawl inside the crystal block, and I'll carry him on my back," said the donkey. "No one will know he's there."

"Yes," shouted Tal with delight. "I can get inside the crystal block."

Noom-Zor-Noom thought for a moment, then he said, "But what will happen, if by any chance I don't open the Door?"

"There's no chance of that," said the donkey. "Animals sometimes know more than men. And I know that you are going to open it."

"If you're that certain," said the old man, "then Tal

can come. But no one must know that he is inside the block."

"No one will," said Tal. "I'll keep perfectly quiet."

So the old man opened the end of the crystal block, and Tal crawled in. There was just enough room for him to lie down, if he curled up with his knees close to his chin. Of course, he was cramped and uncomfortable, but he did not mind that. After Tal had crawled in, Noom-Zor-Noom slid back the end of the block, leaving a small crack for air to pass through. When this was done, he lifted the block up on to the donkey's back and covered it over with the golden cloth. Then he told Millitinkle to go ahead, and together they walked up the long flight of silver stairs.

At the top they came to an ivory gate. On either side of this gate stood two guards. Each of them wore a golden helmet and a golden coat of mail. And each carried a golden lance with a diamond head. When Noom-Zor-Noom came to the gate, the guards stopped him and said, "You are just in time, Noom-Zor-Noom. The stories are to be told to-night. King Tazzarin has ordered us to tell you to go straight to the palace. He has been expecting you back for many days. By now he thinks you are not coming."

Noom-Zor-Noom said, "I have been on a long journey and have gathered my stories. Only with great difficulty did I get back to Troom."

"Then one of the guards said, "What's that on your

donkey's back? Tell us, before we can let you pass. The king wishes us to examine everything that is brought into the city. We must do as we are told."

"That," said Noom-Zor-Noom, "is a block of black crystal. I have written my stories on it, that I might not forget them."

"What do you mean?" said the guards. "We don't understand you."

"I'll show you," said Noom-Zor-Noom. He lifted the cover off one corner of the block and showed the guards how the black surface was covered with golden letters. Then they believed what he said. They asked him no more questions, but made up their minds to let him pass. After telling him to go straight to the palace, they rapped on the gate with their lances, and it opened. And Noom-Zor-Noom and Millitinkle went into Troom.

By that time night had fallen: it was pitch black. But the streets of Troom were paved with colored cobblestones that shone in the dark. Some were red, some were blue, some were yellow, some were green, and some were orange. No matter what color they were, they all shone brilliantly and gave off enough light to illuminate the streets. On either side of the streets were rows of egg-shaped houses. They too shone, each with its own light, so that all of Troom seemed a-blaze with the many colors of the rainbow. It was a wonderful sight. But Tal could not enjoy it, because from the inside of the crystal block he could see nothing.

Noom-Zor-Noom and Millitinkle followed one narrow street after the other. They stopped for nothing; but, turning this way and that, they made their way through the city to the palace. The palace was a huge, egg-shaped building many times as big as any of the other houses. It was gold in color, and it shone like the sun. The windows were made of rubies and gave off a blood red light. In front of the palace was a square, all paved with golden cobble-stones. Around this square stood crowds of people, waiting anxiously to hear what success attended the story-tellers. Just as Noom-Zor-Noom arrived in front of the palace, a man came forth holding a torch in one hand and a scroll in the other. He walked to the middle of the square, and there he stopped. Then the noise of the crowd dwindled to a deathly silence while the man unrolled the scroll and read:

"O People of Troom! Nine years ago to-night my son was carried away from the throne room of the palace. At the time that he was stolen, the Golden Door prophesied and said that when a story was told that would please the Door, then would the Door open and my son, your prince, would be returned. Every year, for eight years, five stories have been told before the Golden Door. But so far none has pleased it. To-night for the ninth time the stories are to be told. If the Door be opened,

*and if my son may be returned, then will happiness
and joy be spread throughout Troom. If the Door
be not opened, then we must continue in sorrow.
And until the time that the Door is opened, no chil-
dren shall be allowed to leave or enter Troom.
This is my order, and by my power as King of
Troom it shall be obeyed."*
　　Signed
　　　KING TAZZARIN OF TROOM.

After reading this proclamation, the man with the
torch returned to the palace. Once more the people began to talk and chatter, and their voices made a great
din. Then Noom-Zor-Noom and Millitinkle pushed
their way through the crowd, crossed the square, and
went to the palace door, where they were met by a
guard, who said, "It is good that you have come, Noom-
Zor-Noom. You are just in time. Leave your donkey
here and follow me."

"I must take my donkey with me," said Noom-Zor-
Noom. "My stories are written on the crystal block she
carries on her back."

"No donkeys are allowed in the palace," said the
guard.

"I can't come without her," said the old man. "If you
won't let her in, I can't read my story."

"I don't know what to do," said the guard. "No one
has ever asked to bring a donkey in before."

"You let me in with her," said Noom-Zor-Noom. "If King Tazzarin is displeased, I shall take the consequences."

So the donkey was allowed to pass. She and Noom-Zor-Noom followed the guard up a flight of golden steps and down a long corridor with diamond walls. At the end they turned into a small room that opened off the throne room. The other four story-tellers were already in this little room: Noom-Zor-Noom was the last to come. When he entered with his donkey, the other men greeted him and said, "We are glad to see you. We thought you were not coming. But why have you got the donkey with you? And what is that on its back?"

"It's a crystal block," said Noom-Zor-Noom. "All the stories I have gathered are written on it."

They said, "You have to tell the story. You cannot read it."

"What difference does it make?" asked Noom-Zor-Noom.

They said, "It depends on what King Tazzarin says. We know that he will only laugh at you, if you go before him with a donkey and a crystal block. He will think you are making a fool of him."

"Why should he?" said Noom-Zor-Noom. "He doesn't care, as long as I open the Door. What else can I do? Tell me, and I'll do it. The block is too heavy to carry. Without the donkey, I could not have got it here at all."

They laughed at the old man, and teased him, and said, "King Tazzarin will think you as stupid as your donkey. He will not even listen to your story. He will have you thrown out of the palace. Take our advice: learn your story by heart. There is still time."

"I will do as I have planned," said Noom-Zor-Noom. "If I am thrown out, it will be my own fault, no one else's." And all the time he thought to himself, "They are afraid that my story is better than theirs. They may as well be, for the story of the giant is going to open the Door. Millitinkle said so."

While the story-tellers were thus talking together in the small room, a trumpet sounded in the throne-room, and King Tazzarin came in. He was a stout man, all dressed in gold and silver robes, and on his head he wore a crown of jewels. His shoes were made of coral, and in the toe of each shoe was set a sparkling, pink diamond. Walking beside him was the queen. She was thin and pale; and all the splendor of her attire only made her face seem more sorrowful and sad. In the many years since her son was stolen away, she had not been seen to smile once. After them came the courtiers and the guards. The king mounted the throne and sat down. And at his feet sat the queen. The courtiers took their places on either side of the throne, and behind them stood the guards, forty on each side of the king. They were dressed the same as the guards at the ivory gate, and each held a lance in one hand, and a tall candle in the

Q

other. These candles they arranged around the throne,
so that the light from them danced and sparkled in the
jewels on the king's crown.

After every one had taken his place, the king said in a
gruff, harsh voice, "Bring me the golden bowl." With
these words that he spoke, one of the guards brought
him a golden bowl and held it before him. Then the
king dropped five gold coins into the bowl and said,
"Carry the bowl in to the story-tellers and let them each
draw a coin. He who draws the coin with the lowest
number on it will tell his story first. He who draws the
highest will come last. The others will come before me
according to their numbers." After the king had finished speaking, the guard made a low bow and went
from the throne-room into the room where the story-
tellers were. There he passed the bowl around, and each
man drew a coin. When they came to compare their
numbers, it was found that Noom-Zor-Noom's was the
highest. The other story-tellers laughed and said, "You
will have to wait until the last. It serves you right for
bringing the donkey. If one of us opens the Door, you
will not have a chance to go before the king; and your
efforts will have been in vain. If we fail, you will see us
thrown into prison, and you will know what fate awaits
you."

Noom-Zor-Noom said, "I am content with my lot. I
shall be able to hear your stories before I tell mine. If
one of you opens the Door, I shall be pleased. If you

don't, I shall still have a chance to open it and free you all from prison. It is good that I should go last."

While they were still talking, a trumpet sounded in the next room, and all became silent, not a sound was to be heard. Then the trumpet sounded again, and the first story-teller knew that his time had come to go before the king. He bade his companions good-bye and walked through the door into the throne-room, where the king, the queen, and the courtiers awaited him.

CHAPTER XV

REPPER-TEP-TEP AND THE STORY OF BANTAGOOMA

THE NAME of the first story-teller was Repper-Tep-Tep. He was a little, short man with a fat, round stomach. On the top of his bald head grew a tuft of gray hairs that stuck straight up in the air. His face was pudgy, and his nose was flat. And his red eyes were set in two narrow slits.

All his life Repper-Tep-Tep had done nothing but tell stories, for he was really too lazy to do much else. Nevertheless, he had learned a great many stories and could tell them well. On this account he had been chosen by the king as one of the men who should try to open the Golden Door. Repper-Tep-Tep did not like this at all. He did not have much courage, and he was afraid of what might happen to him if he should fail. He knew he would have to go to prison. And, to such a lazy man as he was, the idea of being put in prison with no comforts at all, was enough to scare him to death. But, in spite of his fears, he had to tell the story just the same; for what the king commanded had to be done.

He walked straight across the room, and when he got in front of the throne, he made as low a bow as he could;

which was not very low because of his fat stomach. And all the time his legs were shaking so that he could hardly stand up. Then he said in a voice that trembled with fear, "It is your highness's wish that I tell a story. I am greatly honored to have been chosen for such a task. I know what sorrow your highness has suffered since the disappearance of the prince. It is my wish that to-night I may be able to open the Golden Door and return your son to you." Then he bowed again and stayed bowed, until the king spoke.

The king said, "There is a penalty for not opening the Door. You know what it is, don't you?"

"I do," said Repper-Tep-Tep. "But I beg one thing of you: If my story pleases you, you will be merciful and consider that I have done my best?"

A look of anger came over the king's face. He turned to his courtiers and said, "Who is this man, that he should ask for mercy? If there is any reason why he should be treated differently from any one else, tell me, that I may know." And when none of his courtiers answered him or gave him any reason, the king looked squarely down at Repper-Tep-Tep and said, "There will be no mercy shown. Either you will open the Door, or you won't. If you do, you will be rewarded. If you don't, you will be thrown into prison. Such are my orders, and they shall be carried out."

"I know it," said Repper-Tep-Tep, nervously. "I know all that, but . . ."

"There is no 'BUT,'" said the king. "Stop talking and tell your story."

"But . . ." said Repper-Tep-Tep again, for he was really too frightened to know what he was saying.

"If you say that again," roared the king, "I'll have you thrown into prison this minute. Tell us your story."

Then Repper-Tep-Tep drew himself up to his full height and began. At first his voice was unsteady. But soon he forgot all else but the story he was telling. It was the story of

BANTAGOOMA

THERE was an old man who lived all by himself. He had no friends, and he had no name. So the people in the village used to call him Num-Neenam-Fundoo, which means Old-No-Name-Friendless. For many years no one had even seen him, because he never went out of his house. Whenever he wanted to eat, he would give his dog the money and send him off to the market. And there was not a person in the village who did not know Bantagooma, the white dog that belonged to Num-Neenam-Fundoo.

Old Fundoo was a miser. He had lots of money, but he never spent any more than just enough to keep himself alive. The rest of it he kept in a big iron box that was hidden under the kitchen floor. He was so afraid that some one might find out where it was, that he never invited any one to the house. On this account he lost all the friends he used to have when he was young. And he became very lonely and very unhappy.

He was so much of a miser that he never gave his dog any good food. Instead, poor Bantagooma used to eat what his master left on the plate. Then he would curl up in the corner on a dirty old piece of cloth and go to sleep. Often he wished for a nice new bed. Often he dreamed of all kinds of things to eat. But he never complained, for he liked old Fundoo too much.

One evening Bantagooma went to the market to buy his master some supper. When he was coming home with a bag of meat in his mouth, he passed two men standing in the street. One of them said, "There goes Fundoo's dog now. Little does he know what's going to happen to the old man to-night."

"It wouldn't matter if he did," said the other. "Old Fundoo half starves that dog of his. All we'll have to do is give him a little meat, and he won't bother us at all."

Bantagooma pretended to pay no attention. He walked by them and on down the street a little way to where there was a tree. Behind this he dropped his bag and sat down to listen. As he listened, he heard the men talk about how they were going to rob Num-Neenam-Fundoo. That very night they planned to break into his house, find the box of gold, and carry it off. When

Bantagooma heard this, his one thought was to get home and protect his master. So without even thinking to pick up the supper, he ran off home as fast as he could go.

"Where's my supper?" asked Num-Neenam-Fundoo, as soon as the dog came into the house. "What have you done with the money I gave you?"

Then, for the first time, Bantagooma remembered having left the bag behind the tree. He was very much ashamed. He put his paws on Fundoo's knees and licked the old man's hands. He tried in every way he could to let his master know how sorry he was. At the same time he was afraid to run back and get the bag, for fear that the robbers would come while he was away.

"You needn't try to make up to me," said Fundoo, getting angry. "You're a bad dog. I have a mind to beat you."

Bantagooma sat up and begged. He barked and whined. He pawed the spot on the floor under which the gold was buried. He did his best to make Fundoo see what he was worried about, but to no avail.

"You needn't try all those tricks," said the old man. "Where's my supper?"

Bantagooma looked up with big tears in his eyes. He growled just the way he would growl if some one were coming into the house. Again he scratched the floor over the gold. He barked excitedly and bounded around the room.

"Come here!" said Fundoo. "None of this nonsense! What have you done with my supper?"

Bantagooma sat down and wagged his tail.

"Did you buy the meat?" asked Fundoo.

Bantagooma barked twice: that meant "Yes."

"Did you eat it?"

Bantagooma barked once: that meant "no."

"Did some one steal it from you?"

One bark.

"Did you drop it?"

One bark.

"Did you leave it somewhere?"

Two barks.

"What did you do that for?" said Fundoo. "Haven't I told you never to put it down?"

Two barks.

"Then why did you do it?"

Again Bantagooma tried to explain about the robbers.

"Stop that," said Fundoo. "You're a bad dog, and you know you are. Get my supper. When you come back, you can go to bed. Hurry up."

Bantagooma was sad. "I guess there's nothing to do but go," he thought. "Isn't my master stupid not to understand what I mean?" Then he put his tail between his legs and went out of the door.

When he got to the tree, the bag was no longer there. He looked everywhere. He looked behind all the trees up and down the street. The bag had gone. What could he do? Now Fundoo would surely beat him. He wouldn't mind the beating so much, if the old man would only try to understand him. That was more important than the supper. So he ran back home, hoping to find some way of explaining all that had happened.

Fundoo was waiting for him. When he saw the dog come back with nothing in his mouth, he was angry. He picked up a whip and called Bantagooma to him. "You ate the meat yourself! You just tried to fool me. Bad dog! At least I'll teach you to be honest." Without giving poor Bantagooma a chance to say "yes" or "no," he beat him with all his might. "That's a lesson to you. The next time I send you to the market, you won't eat the food." He whipped the dog again. Bantagooma did not whimper. "You're not worth feeding. You're a wretch. Take that!" Fundoo had completely lost his temper. He beat the dog so hard that his arm became tired. Then he kicked him and sent him to bed. "You can stay there for a while!" he said. He tied the dog up with a piece of string and left him in the corner.

All evening long Fundoo paid no attention to Bantagooma. Usually he turned him loose outside to guard the house. But he was too mad even to do that. So, when bed-time came, he left the dog in the kitchen and went upstairs without so much as saying "good night."

As soon as he thought his master had gone to sleep, Bantagooma chewed the string in two and freed himself. He knew that soon the robbers would come. And he had to think of something to do. If he were outside, it would be easy to scare them away. But he had another plan in mind. He wanted to catch them and hold them so that Fundoo might see how much he knew. Then, perhaps, his master would forgive him. Quietly he tiptoed upstairs, and one by one he brought his master's clothes down. He put them all on and sat down in the chair by the fire. There he waited, pretending that he was asleep. Pretty soon he heard two men talking outside the door.

"Bantagooma must be off hunting," one of them said. "Fundoo always puts him out at night. If he were anywhere round, he'd bark at us."

"I'm just as glad he isn't here," said the other.

The next minute the door was pried open, and in came the two robbers. They each had a gun, and one of them carried a lantern. Bantagooma sat very still right where he was.

"Sh!" said one of the robbers, looking at the figure in the chair. "There's old Fundoo asleep in the chair. If he wakes up, we'll shoot him. If not, so much the better for us."

"The gold is somewhere under the floor," said the one with the lantern. "Come, let us look for it."

They got down on their hands and knees, and tapped the floor here and there, listening for a hollow place. At last they found it. They pulled up the boards, and there they saw the box of gold. In their excitement they both put their guns down and tugged at the box to get it out. After they had lifted it up, instead of going off with it, they opened it to count the money. Bantagooma watched for his chance. When he was certain that they were off their guard, he jumped up and barked and growled furiously. The men were so surprised and so frightened that they ran for the door. But Bantagooma headed them off and drove them into a corner, where they stood trembling with fear, while the dog snarled and snapped at their legs.

"Here, Bantagooma," said one, "take this and let us go." Out of his pocket he took the bag of meat that the dog had left behind the tree and threw it at him. Bantagooma paid no attention; he only went on growling and barking. "Your master will whip you for taking his clothes," said the other. "You had better be quiet and let us go." But nothing they said made any difference to the dog. He kept on barking and growling for all he was worth.

Old Fundoo, hearing the noise, woke up and lit his lamp. He looked for his clothes; they were gone. "I have been robbed of everything," he said. And he jumped out of bed and ran downstairs in his white nightgown. When he came into the kitchen and saw the box of gold in the middle of the floor, he knew at once what had happened. The next minute he saw the two robbers huddled in the corner. He did not wait to say a word, but he picked up one of the guns and called the dog off.

Then he aimed the gun at the robbers and said, "I am going to shoot you. You deserve it, for trying to rob me."

"Please don't," said the robbers. "Do anything else you wish, but don't shoot us."

"Tell me who you are," said Fundoo. "Why did you try to rob me?"

Then the robbers told him all, even about how Bantagooma had dropped the meat. They went on and said, "We heard that you had a great deal of gold hidden under the floor. So we decided to steal it. When we came into the house, we thought we saw you asleep in the chair. But it was not you, it was your dog dressed in your clothes. The dog caught us and drove us into the corner. We did not dare move, for fear that he would bite us. That's what happened to us. That's how we were caught."

Fundoo said, "I won't shoot you this time. I shall keep you prisoners to-night, and in the morning I'll take you to jail." He bound the robbers hand and foot with a rope. Then he gave Bantagooma a big bowl of bread and milk. And all that night he and the dog sat in the kitchen guarding their prisoners.

The next morning Fundoo took the robbers to the jail. When he came back, he said to Bantagooma, "You saved me from being robbed last night. I am sorry I scolded you and did not understand about the meat. Tell me whatever you want, and I'll give it to you."

With these words that Fundoo spoke, Bantagooma ran over and barked at the box of gold.

"What could you do with that?" asked Fundoo, for he had no idea that the dog would ask for his money. "You don't want it, do you?"

"Yes," barked Bantagooma.

Since the old man had made the promise, he had to keep it. He opened the box and told the dog that the money was his. Bantagooma took it, a mouthful at a time, and carried most of it to the market place. There he bought everything that was needed for a feast. And he spent the whole day carrying the food back to the house. When Fundoo saw so much food, he thought the dog had gone mad. But Bantagooma made his master understand that he was to set to work and cook it all. While Fundoo was busy doing this, the dog went to the houses of all the nice people in the village. Outside of each house he stood and barked until the people came to see what he wanted. Then he got them to follow him. From house to house he went, and soon a great crowd was trailing behind him, wondering where he would lead them. After getting every one he wanted, he led the crowd to his master's house. There Num-Neenam-Fundoo had prepared a feast such as a king would have. The people came in and ate and enjoyed themselves. Old Fundoo entertained them with stories about his dog. They all thought the old man so kind and so generous, that thereafter they came to see him more and more often. In this way Num-Neenam-Fundoo made a great many friends, just as many as any one else in the village had. Thus, though he did not have much money, he had a great deal of happiness. And he and Bantagooma are alive to-day and are the best of friends.

NO SOONER had Repper-Tep-Tep finished his story, than he looked at the Golden Door to see whether it was going to open or not. And all the others did the same. However, though they waited in silence a long time for something to happen, nothing did. The Door remained fast shut: it showed no sign of opening. At last the king said, "He has told a good story, but so have many others. He has failed to open the Door. Take him and throw him into prison."

"Please, your highness, grant me mercy," cried Repper-Tep-Tep, kneeling down at the foot of the throne. "I don't want to go to prison."

"I know you don't," said the king. "Neither does any one else."

"Please . . . please . . . don't," he sobbed, crying like a child. "I have done all I could. Be merciful!"

But the more Repper-Tep-Tep begged and pleaded, the more angry the king grew. He turned to the guards and said, "This man is no sight for me to see. Take him and throw him into prison!"

Immediately two guards rushed forward and seized poor Repper-Tep-Tep. They dragged him out of the room and down the hall. And as they went further and further away with him, his voice could still be heard, crying, "Please . . . please . . . don't throw me into prison! Be merciful!" They took him on down a flight of stairs to the bottom of the palace, where they opened a trap door and threw him headlong into a dungeon. Then the guards went back to the throne-room and stood by the king just as if nothing at all had happened.

CHAPTER XVI

BRAH AND THE STORY OF TARRANDAR'S SECRET

FROM THE ROOM where they were, all the other story-tellers could hear just what had happened to Repper-Tep-Tep. And when, at last, his screams had died away down the hall, the oldest of the story-tellers turned to Noom-Zor-Noom and said, "The king is in a bad humor to-night. You had better not risk going before him with the donkey. There is no telling what he may do."

"Let him do what he pleases," said Noom-Zor-Noom. "I am only doing the best I can."

"I know that," said the man, whose name was Brah. "But you see what happened to Repper-Tep-Tep. He, too, was doing the best he could."

"But it wasn't very good," said Noom-Zor-Noom. "He shouldn't have behaved the way he did."

"Then you know how to behave better?" asked Brah with a laugh.

"Yes," said Noom-Zor-Noom. "I hope I do."

"Then I'm surprised you even think of going before the king with a donkey. He won't stand for it a minute," said Brah. "I only say this because I want to help you. As for myself, I don't care what happens to me. I am too old to be worried by the thought of going

R

to prison. But you will just make a fool of yourself."

Hardly had the man finished these words, when the trumpet sounded . . . once . . . twice. And Brah, the second story-teller, knew that his time had come to go before the king.

He was a tall thin man; and he was so old and bent that he leaned on two canes when he walked. In his long life he had heard a great many stories, and for this reason he had been chosen by Tazzarin to try to open the Golden Door. When he heard the trumpet sound, he thought to himself, "I am old and have not much life left. It makes little difference whether I go to prison or not." He showed no signs of fear and he did not tremble, but he went before the king calmly and quietly. He bowed his head and he spoke to the king with great respect. He said, "O king, in my long life I have heard many stories. This one that I am going to tell to-night is the best of all I have heard. It may open the Door, and it may not. But in either case I am happy to have been honored with such a task as you have set before me."

The king heard these words and said to the queen, "I like this old man. I hope he will succeed." Then he turned to Brah and said, "We are ready to hear your story. May you succeed! If you don't, you must suffer the same penalty as the others."

Brah said nothing. He bowed his head and raised it. Then in a low, even voice, he began the story of

TARRANDAR'S SECRET

IN A far-off country called Besh lived a king named Tarrandar. For ninety years he had been king, so that no one in Besh knew of any other ruler but Tarrandar. All his people loved him, because he ruled them well and made them happy. And every one dreaded the day when this good king would rule no more.

Tarrandar was old. He had a long white beard and silvery hair. And when he walked he leaned on a cane, for his legs were stiff and his back bent. So he spent most of his time sitting in the palace, where he looked after the welfare of his people and did all he could to make Besh the happiest kingdom in the world. But his mind was troubled, for he had no son. He did not know who would take care of his country, after he was too old to rule. This worried him much and made him very, very unhappy.

One day, as he sat wondering about the future, he remembered a secret his father had told him. The old man had said:

"Tarrandar, should you have no son, remember the scroll. It is hidden behind a stone in the tower. Touch it not, unless you have no children. If you have children and touch it, then you will die. And the kings of Besh shall rule no more."

It was so long ago that his father had told him this, that Tarrandar had forgotten most of what he said. While he thought about it, more and more came back to his mind: The scroll had been put in the tower wall by the first king of Besh. Ever since, for over a thousand years, it had lain there untouched by any king. All of the kings knew of it, but none had needed to consult it. The secret had been carefully kept and only passed on from father to son; for if the secret had become known to any one else, the charm of the scroll would be broken. This much Tarrandar knew. But what the charm was and what was written on the scroll, neither Tarrandar nor any other king could say.

At last Tarrandar decided to consult the scroll. One night, after every one in the palace had gone to bed, he took a lantern and started up the tower stairs. They were narrow and steep and wound up and up like a corkscrew. Every few steps Tarrandar had to stop, for his legs grew tired and he was out of breath. Finally he reached the top and entered a small round room. It had nothing in it but a bed; and the walls were made of blocks of blue stone. When Tarrandar held up his lantern to look at the bed, he saw that the blankets and sheets reflected everything just like a mirror. So he set the lantern on the bed, and the light was scattered all over the room. Then he set to work to look for the scroll. Round and round he went rapping each stone with the end of his cane. Rap, rap, rap, rap, rap. All the stones sounded the same, solid and hard. Again he went round. Rap, rap, rap, rap, rap, rap. This time he thought he found one that sounded a bit hollow. So he struck it again to make sure. Then he struck the one next to it so as to compare the sounds. After this he was satisfied that there was a difference. So he pressed the palm of his hand flat against the stone to feel it. What was his surprise when his hand stuck. He started to pull it away, and the stone swung open like a little door. There, right before his eyes, was a golden scroll, lying in the hole all tied up with silver ribbon. He took it out, untied it and unrolled it, and spread it out on a bed by the lantern. On it, written in beautiful jeweled letters, was this:

Ali Mali Beshi
Karanda! Karanda! Karanda!
Meshi Troo Meegum
Eena Stella
Eena Deema
Eena Kreska
Meshi Agga Loonta
Aggacha

In our language it means:

Oh, Childless King of Besh,
Greetings! Greetings! Greetings!
Take Three Snow Flakes
One a Star
One a Diamond
One a Crescent
Take Water from the River Loonta
Drink

Tarrandar learned the writing by heart, then he put the scroll back where he had found it. He pushed the stone into place, took his lantern, and went back down the stairs.

For many days and many nights Tarrandar pondered over what he had read. He could see but one meaning in it: he was to mix the snow flakes with the water and drink. But where he was to get the snow flakes, and how he was to get the water, were questions he could not answer. There was a river called Loonta. But it was so far away and so high up in the mountains that few people had ever been there. He knew the river ran through snow and ice: he didn't know what shapes the snow flakes were. Even if they were the right shapes, how could they be brought back to him without melting? He couldn't go to where they were; he was too old and too weak. At last, after much thought, he decided to send men to the river Loonta to see what they could see. So he called together the bravest in all the kingdom and spoke his wish. When the men heard it, they were sad, for they did not think it possible to carry out Tarrandar's wish. But they loved him so much, that they said they would go. Tarrandar fitted out a hundred men with all they could possibly need and sent them off to the Loonta.

For a whole year no word was heard from the men. Finally they came back, thin and worn out. They told the king they had seen the river. It was all purple and so cold that none of them could go near it, to say nothing of getting the water. As for the snow flakes, they had found every shape but the three the king wanted.

When the king heard this, he was sad; he did not know what to do. So he called for more men and again sent a hundred off. They went away for a year, and came back with news that they had found some star-shaped flakes. But they couldn't bring them back, because they melted. Then the king sent off a hundred more. They found the diamond-shaped flakes, but were not able to bring *them* back. Finally a hundred more men went and came back with the news that they had found the crescent-shaped flakes. So Tarrandar knew the snow flakes could be had, if only some way might be devised of getting them back before they melted.

Already four years had passed by and Tarrandar was becoming very, very old. And he had wasted so much money fitting out the men, that his people began to think him mad. They could not understand what on earth he wanted of the snow flakes and the water. "He is getting old and foolish," they said. "He will waste all the money in the kingdom before he is through." They began to grumble and complain. They refused to pay any more attention to his requests; and no men offered themselves to go to the Loonta.

But Tarrandar was not to be discouraged. He called for his goldsmith and said to him, "Make me a big gold jug, just as big as a man can carry. When you make the stopper, make it of gold too. Only hollow it out and make a lid for it, so that it will be like a box. But it must fit the neck of the jug exactly. This you do, and have it ready for me to-morrow." The goldsmith obeyed the king's orders. All day and all night he worked. And by the next morning he had made just such a jug with just such a stopper as Tarrandar had asked for.

Without saying a word to any one, Tarrandar took the jug, put it on his shoulder, and went out of the palace. When the people of Besh saw their king walking through the street burdened with a heavy load, they ran up to him and said, "O king, what is the matter that you must carry so heavy a load? You are too old for such work. Let us help you."

Tarrandar said, "I have asked men to go to the Loonta, and they refused. Now I am going myself. It is only for your own good that I want what I want."

When the people heard this, they were ashamed. They thought that if Tarrandar went away, he would never come back. They said, "As many men as you want will go to the Loonta. Only you stay here. We cannot live without you."

The king said, "As you wish, so I shall do. But I want a thousand men to go to the Loonta. Nine hundred of these are to carry wood as near the Loonta as possible. There they are to build a fire, so that the other hundred men may be kept warm while they go to the river's edge and fill this jug with water. After the jug is

filled, let them get the snow flakes and put them inside
the stopper. The cold of the water will keep the flakes
from melting. This is what I want done. Will you
do it?"

Straightway a thousand men offered themselves to go.
The king gave them the jug, fitted them out, and sent
them off. A year later they returned with their task
done. Everything the king wished for, they brought
back. The water was in the jug, and the snow flakes
were in the gold stopper. When Tarrandar saw this, he
was very happy. He thanked the men for all they had
done and promised them they would be rewarded.

Tarrandar's first thought was to have the jug taken
up to the tower room. But he did not dare ask any one
to do it, lest his secret should be found out. So in the
night he tried to lift the jug himself. But the water
had made it so heavy that he could hardly move it, let
alone carry it up-stairs. However, after a great deal of
work, he lifted it up one step. There he had to leave
it, for he was so tired he could do no more. From then
on, night after night, Tarrandar moved his jug one step
higher. All the time the people of Besh were becoming
anxious to know what had been the purpose of his sending men to the Loonta. And all the time Tarrandar was
becoming older and weaker. But he stuck to his task
and struggled with the jug, and no one knew what
agony the poor old king went through every night. At
last he neared the top. Then his strength failed him,

and for nearly a month he had to be content to leave the jug where it was. He thought he would never reach his goal. Finally he did, however, and with one last effort he lifted the jug into the room and slid it over by the bed. Then he went down stairs, too tired to do anything that night, but his mind made up that on the morrow he would learn the secret of the scroll.

At midnight the next night Tarrandar, lantern in hand, mounted to the tower room. He looked everywhere for the scroll; it had gone. He tried to remember everything that had been written on it, and a voice in the room whispered the words to him. Then there was a dead silence. He looked around, but could see no one. So he sat down on the bed and took the golden stopper out of the jug. He opened it and found the snow flakes all there. He poured some purple water out of the jug on to them. At once they melted, and the water became warm. Next, he put the golden stopper to his lips and drank. With the first swallow he became very sleepy. And by the time he had taken three swallows, he fell back on the bed and went sound asleep.

When Tarrandar woke up his lantern had burned out, and the sun was shining in the windows of the round room. At first he did not know where he was, or what had happened to him. He felt for his beard: it had gone. Stranger still, all his clothes seemed so big and loose. Instead of being old and stiff, he could move his legs freely and easily. There were no wrinkles in his skin, no aches in his joints. In fact he felt a great desire to run and jump. Then he remembered that the clothes on the bed acted like mirrors. So he rolled over and looked at himself in the pillow. One look was enough to show him that he had turned into a boy again. His hair was yellow and his cheeks were red. And in his eyes was that same twinkle he used to have when young. He jumped up from the bed and ran downstairs as fast as he could. When the people in the palace saw him, they all knew that Tarrandar had turned into a boy. The news spread throughout the kingdom. And all the people in the land of Besh rejoiced, happy in the thought that their good king Tarrandar could begin to rule all over again.

WHEN Brah came to the end of his story, he looked up and knew that the king and queen had been greatly pleased. He could see by their faces that they still hoped there was more of the story to be told. So he said, "That is the end: King Tarrandar became a boy and began to rule all over again. So the people of Besh continued to be happy."

The king said, "It is too bad that your story has ended. I wish there were more. I like it."

The queen sighed and said, "So do I. How fortunate the people of Besh were to have their king grow young again."

Brah said nothing. He stood still with his head down

and his eyes on the floor. The king and the queen and the courtiers watched for the Door to open, for they really hoped that the story of Tarrandar's Secret might be successful. But the longer they waited, the clearer it became that Brah had failed. He knew this as well as the others. After a while he looked up at the king and said, "I have failed, just as the others have failed. Tell the guards to take me."

"The Door may open yet," said the king, hopefully. "Let us wait a little longer and see."

"No," said Brah. "There's no use. It must be that I am too old to know what kind of a story a child would like."

"I don't think so," said the king. "That story of yours should please any one."

"But it hasn't pleased the Door," said Brah. "Let me go to prison."

"What!" said the king. "You want to go to prison!"

"It makes no difference," said Brah. "My life is nearly done with anyhow. I may as well die in prison."

When the king heard in what way Brah spoke, he felt sorry for the old man. In his own heart he would have liked to have shown him mercy. But this he could not do. So he ordered the guards to take Brah away. And they took him away and cast him into the dungeon.

CHAPTER XVII

AKADON AND THE STORY OF THE TOY MAKER

WHILE Brah was going off to prison, Akadon, the third story-teller, said to Noom-Zor-Noom, "No wonder those men have failed. Such stories as they tell would never open the Door. My story will do it."

Noom-Zor-Noom said, "You are very sure. Do you think that your story is so much better than theirs?"

"I don't think it is, I *know* it is," said Akadon. "I have not even thought of going to prison. If the king had called on me the first year, he wouldn't have had to wait so long for the Door to open."

Noom-Zor-Noom smiled to himself and said, "I hope you are right. It will be a wonderful thing if you are."

Then the trumpet sounded twice, and Akadon went into the throne-room. He walked boldly up to the throne, for he was a big man and knew no fear. He was dressed in blue pantaloons and a silver jacket, and around his waist was tied a golden sash. He did not even bow to the king; but straightway he said, "O King, the story that I am about to tell will please the Door. It is a story that no one but me has ever heard. If it does not bring back your son, then you may know that no story will ever open the Golden Door."

When King Tazzarin heard Akadon's boast, he scowled and said, "You speak boldly. It may be that you think too much of yourself."

"It's not that," said Akadon, in no way upset by the king's words. "It's only that I know a good story when I hear one. And I know that mine is the best."

"That remains to be seen," said the king. "If you speak the truth, you shall be well rewarded. If not, you must go to prison."

"As you have ordered, so it shall be done," said Akadon. "But before beginning my story, I have a request to make."

"If you are going to beg for mercy," said the king, "I'll tell you right now that you are wasting your time."

"I'm not," said Akadon. "I don't want mercy. I have not even thought of going to prison, so sure am I that my story will open the Door."

"Then what do you wish?" asked the king, slightly taken back by the man's boldness. "Tell me!"

"When my story is done, let me rap three times on the Golden Door," said Akadon. "In that way I shall be able to make it open. That is all I ask."

"That's a good deal," said the king. "It's more than I have granted to any of the other story-tellers."

"But none of the others have asked to do it," said Akadon. "They don't know as much as I do."

The king leaned back and thought for a moment. Then he spoke to the queen and to some of the courtiers. And they said that the man was too bold to have his wish granted. But the king, who was willing that anything should be tried, granted the man his wish. Then Akadon, in a voice that was loud and full of confidence, told the story of the

TOY MAKER

OLD NEE-FOO spent his life making toys. He had a shop, and all day long he sat in the window carving and painting. He made wooden dolls, wooden animals, wooden boats, and every other kind of toy that the children liked. He never had much money, for often he would give his toys away to poor children. But he loved his work and he loved every toy that he made.

No one really knew much about old Nee-Foo. Of course, he could be seen all day sitting in his shop. But what he did at night and where he went on holidays, no one knew. He had never been seen after dark, and people who went to his shop on holidays never found him there. For this reason there was much talk about Nee-Foo. Of course, nothing bad was ever said about him, for all knew that the old man would never do harm to any one. Just the same the people who lived in the village would have given a great deal to know the truth. Some said that he was a magician, and that at night he turned himself into an animal. Others thought he had a secret room in his shop, where he could hide himself and sleep. And there were those who said that he was just like any one else: it was all untrue that he could not be found. But old Nee-Foo himself kept his mouth very tight shut, he never answered any questions about anything but his toys.

One morning the children in the village, when they went by Nee-Foo's shop, saw the old man sitting there as usual. But he was not working, for one arm was all tied up in pieces of white cloth. This made them wonder. One of them went into the shop and said, "What's the matter, Nee-Foo? What have you done to your arm?"

Nee-Foo sighed and said, "My arm is broken. It will be a long time before I can make any more toys."

The little boy said, "How did it happen? Did you fall?"

Nee-Foo said, "My toys are a part of myself."

The boy, hearing this, did not ask any more questions. He went out and told the other children what the toy maker had said. And none of the children understood. So they ran and asked their mothers and fathers. But no one in the whole village knew what Nee-Foo meant by "My toys are a part of myself." The people thought that Nee-Foo had been in a fight and had had his arm broken. That was all they thought, nothing more.

s

They looked around for the person with whom he fought. They could not find any one. So they wondered more than ever what the toy maker did with himself at night.

Nee-Foo got well and started making toys again. Then all the children were happy. For many months he went on making toys. People began to forget about what had happened to him. They might have forgotten altogether, except that something more happened. A man went to Nee-Foo's to buy a toy for his boy. He did not see Nee-Foo sitting in the window, so he knocked at the door. No one answered. He pushed the door open, and there, on the floor, he found Nee-Foo hardly able to move. He looked at the old man and said, "What's happened to you? You look as if you had been beaten and stamped on. Tell me who has harmed you. I'll see that they are punished."

Nee-Foo said in a weak voice, "I am badly hurt. It will be a long time before I can make any more toys."

The man said, "Who hurt you?"

Nee-Foo said, "My toys are a part of myself."

When the man heard this, he did not know what Nee-Foo meant. He thought the old man was out of his mind. He left Nee-Foo and went for the doctor. Together they fixed the old man up and made him as comfortable as possible. But he told them nothing more than he had said in the first place. And to all their questions, he said, "My toys are a part of myself."

The man went among his friends, and to every one he met he told the story about Nee-Foo. He said, "I found him lying in his shop all bruised and beaten. When I asked him what was the matter and what had happened, he said, 'My toys are a part of myself.' Now what do you think he means by those words? There is no one in the village who would harm the toy maker. We all like him too much. Twice this has happened. I can't understand it." These words he spoke to his friends. And no one could understand them.

One man said, "I think he must go to some other part of the world at night. He has probably got enemies there."

Another said, "There was a dog fight last night. Nee-Foo turns into a dog at night. That's what has happened to him."

Many people had ideas, but not one of them really knew the truth. They talked about this and that, and each one thought he knew it all. They watched Nee-Foo closely, hoping to see what he did after dark. All they could see was that he closed his shop and lit no lamp. But where he went and what he did, still remained as much of a mystery as ever.

Again the toy maker got well. He made many toys and seemed very happy. The children crowded around his window and watched him. The months passed by, soon it would be Christmas. The boys and girls in the village stopped at his shop to pick out the things they wanted for presents. Nee-Foo talked with them and told them stories.

A week before Christmas the people in the village had a holiday. No one did any work. The shop keepers closed their shops, the blacksmith let his fire go out, and the men did no work in the fields. Even Nee-Foo took a rest.

The day after the holiday, every one went to buy toys at Nee-Foo's. One after another stopped at the shop, but no one could get in. The door was locked. They peeped through the window, the shop was empty. So they turned away and thought no more about it. "How foolish he is," they said. "He should know that we want toys for Christmas. He has probably gone off and is having a good time somewhere. He will be back to-morrow."

On the next day the shop was still closed. The people became alarmed; they were afraid they could get no toys for Christmas. And when on the third day, there was still no sign of the toy maker, the people in the village began to talk. Men began to look for Nee-Foo. But no one could be found who had seen him since before the holiday. A house to house search was made, but to no avail. At last they gave up all hope, and decided that there would be no toys for Christmas.

Now not far from the village, near a river, there lived a little girl. She was poor and had always wished for toys, but her mother and father could get her none. So she lived without toys and amused herself as best she could. Often in the afternoon she went to the bank of the river and floated pieces of wood in the water and threw stones at them. In this way she passed much time playing. About a week after Nee-Foo had been missed, this girl went to play by the river. As she stood there throwing stones, she thought she saw something floating down with the current. She waited till it came near, then she threw stones beyond it to bring it to shore. At last she got hold of it, and what was it but the body of a doll with only one leg and one arm. She picked it up, dried it off, and put it down on some grass. "I wonder where the other leg and arm are," she thought. "Perhaps if I wait here, they too will float by." So she waited. Bye and bye the arm floated into sight, and not long after it came the leg. The little girl rescued them both. Then she picked up all the parts and ran to the house. She said to her mother, "Look what I've found. I found them floating in the river."

Her mother looked and saw that all the parts belonged to the same doll. She said, "Some child has broken its doll and thrown it away. It's too bad Nee-Foo isn't here. He could fix it for you. Then you'd have a toy."

The girl said, "I don't see how anybody could treat a doll so badly. I'm going to keep it and get Father to fix it. Then I'll make a dress for it. And it will be mine."

As she wished, so her father did. He fixed the doll as

well as he could and gave it back to his child. The girl took it and at once started to make a dress. All the rest of the afternoon she worked with a thread and needle. By evening she had made a beautiful dress for the doll and put it on. She took care of the doll as if it were a child. That night when she went to bed, she took it with her and made a nice, soft bed for it under the blankets. There the doll slept, and the little girl was very happy.

The next morning, when the people went to look for Nee-Foo, they found him at work in his shop. They said to him, "Where have you been all this time? Didn't you know that we would want toys for Christmas?"

Nee-Foo said, "I don't know whether to make any more toys or not."

They said, "What do you mean?"

Nee-Foo said, "My toys are a part of myself."

This time the people thought that there must be something in what he said, because now for the third time, he gave them the same answer. So they said, "Tell us what you mean by, 'My toys are a part of myself'! We cannot understand you."

Nee-Foo said, "If you didn't understand me the first time, you won't understand me now."

"How are we going to find out," they asked, "if you won't tell us?" And they begged him to tell them just what he meant. At last the old man said, "You go and call all the children in the village and bring them here. Then I will tell what I mean."

So all the children in the village were gathered together and brought to the toy maker's shop. There they crowded around him, while he spoke thus:

"My toys are a part of myself. By that I mean that whenever one of my toys is broken or badly taken care of, it is just as if I had been hurt. Every night, after closing the shop, I turn myself into a toy, one of the ones I have sold. That's what happens to me. The first night I turned into a little wooden boy doll. The child that owned me got angry and smashed the arm of his doll. That's why you saw me the next day with a broken arm.

"Later I turned into another doll and went to the house of a little girl. She got angry at her mother and stamped on her toys. That was why I was all bruised and beaten in the morning.

"On the holiday, some child pulled a leg and an arm off his toy and threw it into the river. I happened to be in that toy. After being broken and thrown into the river, it was impossible for me to come back. That's why I stayed away so long. But a kind little girl saved me, put me together, and took the best of care of me. So I was able to come back.

"That's what I meant, when I said, 'My toys are a part of myself.'"

When the children heard this, they were sorry for the

way they had mistreated their toys. And they promised Nee-Foo never to be bad to them again. So he set to work and made lots and lots of new toys for Christmas. And to the little girl who had saved him from the river he gave the choice of as many toys in his shop as she wished.

As AKADON told the last words of the story, he turned and spoke them to the Golden Door. He spoke them slowly and in such a way that he seemed to expect the Door to fling open at any moment. When it did not open, he walked over to it and struck it heavily with his fist. Again he struck it with all his strength. And when he struck it for the third time, he shouted, "I command you to open! It is Akadon's story that you have heard." But the Door paid no heed to his words. It remained as fast shut as it always had been. Then Akadon turned to the king and said, "Give it time: it will open."

The king waited as long as he saw fit. Then he said angrily, "You are a boaster. You have said much but done little."

"Give it time," said Akadon. "It will open, if you only wait."

"Wait!" said the king with an ill-humored laugh. "I have waited long enough already."

"Just a minute more," pleaded Akadon. "Give me a chance."

"You are a fool to think you know so much," said the king. And with these words, the king and the queen and courtiers all laughed and jeered at Akadon. They called him a boaster; they called him a fool; and they told him that he deserved what was coming to him.

Akadon grew red in the face and was covered with confusion. Two or three times he began to speak, but no one stopped laughing long enough to listen to his words. "I tell you . . . I tell you . . . It's going to open," he shouted. "My story is the best." And he stood in front of the throne trying to make himself heard.

At last the king called for silence. Then he said to Akadon, "You have done worse than fail. You have proved yourself a boaster. It's such as you that not only waste my time, but the time of every one else. It will be well for the Kingdom of Troom to be rid of you." With these words that he spoke, the king called to the guards;

and they rushed forward and seized Akadon. He begged and pleaded of the king to wait longer. But the king only jeered at him, as did all the courtiers. The guards carried Akadon out of the room. And all the way down the hall his voice could be heard, as he screamed and protested and said that he knew his story would open the Golden Door.

CHAPTER XVIII

PUNDA-POO AND THE STORY OF THE FOUR WINDS

PUNDA-POO was a thin little man with a hump on his back. He looked like a mouse, and he hardly ever said a word, but he always listened. In this way he heard many things. And whatever he heard he remembered. So, though he never told any stories, he knew quite a few. And it had always been said of Punda-Poo that if he could be made to talk, he would tell of the most wonderful things in the world. But no one had ever heard him tell a story. So no one really knew.

Ever since King Tazzarin had ordered him to be one of the story-tellers, Punda-Poo had been horrified at the thought of talking before so many people. And now, when he heard the trumpet sound and knew that his turn had come, he said to Noom-Zor-Noom, "This is a thousand times worse than being put into prison. I wish they would cast me right into the dungeon without making me tell a story. There is no use of my talking, I cannot open the Door."

"You may be able to," said Noom-Zor-Noom. "They say you can tell of wonderful things."

"So they say," said Punda-Poo. "But they don't know."

"Just the same, you'd better hurry in," said Noom-Zor-Noom. "The king is waiting for you."

So Punda-Poo went into the throne-room, muttering to himself, "I'd be much better off if I kept quiet. If I talk, I'll get into trouble." He shuffled across the room and stopped in front of the throne. There he made a little bow, and then he stood up as straight as he could. And any one seeing him must have felt sorry for him, he looked so miserable and small in front of the big throne and all the people who were staring at him.

"Tell us your name!" said the king in a gruff, angry voice.

"Punda-Poo," said the man.

"Is that the only name you have?" asked the king.

"No, your highness," said Punda-Poo. "I have another. But pray don't make me tell it."

"Why not?" asked the king.

"I don't want to, your highness," said Punda-Poo. "I don't like it."

"All the more reason why you should tell it," said the king. "But if you don't want to, I will." And when Punda-Poo made no answer, the king went on and said, "This man is called The Mouse. He is so shy and keeps so much out of people's way that he is seldom seen and never heard. No one has ever heard him tell a story.

But it is said that he can tell of marvelous things. Is that true, Mouse?"

"I don't know, your highness," said Punda-Poo in a high, squeaky voice. And he was too embarrassed to look up from the floor.

"Whether it's true or not," said the king, "we'll soon find out."

"Yes, your highness," said Punda-Poo.

"Any how," said the king to the courtiers, "we shall hear The Mouse talk. That in itself will be wonderful." Then he looked down at Punda-Poo. "Tell us your story, Mouse," he said. "And if you don't open the Golden Door, you must go to prison with the others. But you won't mind it there so much. They say that mice like dark places and aren't used to eating much."

Punda-Poo said nothing. He waited for a moment; then he began to tell the story of

THE FOUR WINDS

A GREAT EMPEROR and empress had two children, one a prince, the other a princess. The prince was strong and healthy; he rode horseback, he went hunting, and he flew kites. The princess was not so strong; she had been sick a good deal when she was a baby. On this account the empress saw to it that the girl was watched

with care. She did not let her do this, she did not let
her do that; and everywhere the princess went, some
one went with her. Of course the poor girl hated all
this. For how could she get strong, unless she was allowed to do things? But if she ever complained, her
mother always said, "It's all for your own good, Neea.
When you grow up you'll understand. Just do what I
tell you to, and everything will be all right."

Because she was supposed to be delicate and because
she was always with them, the emperor and empress
grew very fond of Neea. They petted her, they gave her
presents, and they waited on her all the time. Soon it
got so that each one was trying to do nicer things for
her than the other. If the empress gave the girl a present, the emperor gave her a bigger present the next day.
So it went. One day the princess asked for a new dress.
At once the empress ordered a dress made for her daughter. And the emperor, not to be outdone by his wife,
had one made too. But his was a little bit more beautiful than the one the empress gave. After that not a day
passed but one of them gave Neea a new dress. And
each day the dresses became more fluffy and more silky.
This went on, until in the end the empress gave the girl
such a dress as you have never seen. It was all made out
of silvery silk and lace. And the skirt had thousands
of ruffles, one over the other, so that it reached down to
her ankles and floated around her like a silver bell. With
it came a shawl that was itself big enough to make a

Merry Christmas

Wishing you a blessed and
joyful holiday!
The Baldwins 2012
Billy, Maggie, Tommy, Sean
Marcia & Todd

dress. It too was of silk and was all embroidered with pearls. These the empress gave to her daughter and said, "Put on this new dress. When you've got it on, we'll go for a walk in the garden. It's warm to-day, and the sun will be good for you."

So Neea put on the new dress. She took her mother's hand, and together they went out into the garden. There, as they strolled up and down, the empress saw a flower she wanted to pick. She let go of the girl's hand and leaned over to pick the flower. Just then a strong puff of wind came. It caught Neea's skirt; it caught her shawl. And before the empress could do anything or say a word, the girl was lifted off her feet and carried high up in the air. The empress shouted and called for help. Her husband came running out of the palace. He said, "What's the matter, that you shout so? What has happened?"

The empress said, "What has happened! Look up there and you'll see."

The emperor looked up and saw a tiny white speck in the sky. He said, "What is it? A cloud?"

The empress said, "It's Neea. The wind caught in her dress and carried her away."

Then the emperor scolded his wife, as if that would help bring the girl back. While he scolded, Neea floated out of sight altogether; she could be seen no more.

The wind kept blowing the princess up and up. Soon she could not see the earth at all. Everywhere she looked she saw nothing but blue sky. Finally in the distance she saw some land. The wind blew her over this land. Then she began to come down. Down and down she dropped, until, with almost no jar at all, she landed gently on her feet. She was standing in the middle of a great plain. As far as she could see, there were no trees, no grass, no living thing of any kind. The ground was as flat as a table and all covered with fine blue sand that was hard and smooth. No wind at all was blowing, and the sun was very hot.

"This is a strange place," thought Neea. "I wonder where I am. There must be people here, if I can only find them." But she did not know in which direction to go, everything looked so much the same. However, she made up her mind to walk. She went as far as she went, and still she saw nothing but the flat, blue plain. Yet she kept on going, until she saw what she thought might be a house. When she came near it, it was a house, but different from any other house she had ever seen. It was all blue, just the color of the sand. And instead of being on the ground, it was on the top of a high blue pole. As she stood looking at it, a puff of wind blew, and the whole house swung around so that it faced the wind, the same as a weather vane does. Without thinking, Neea blew at the house. It turned toward her, the front door opened, and an old hag stuck her head out. She had long gray hair, and her face was all wrinkled and pale. She said, "What do you want that you come

AND BEFORE THE EMPRESS COULD DO ANYTHING OR SAY A WORD, THE
GIRL WAS LIFTED OFF HER FEET AND CARRIED HIGH UP IN THE AIR.

T

to the home of the winds. If my daughters find you here, they'll do you harm."

"It's not my fault that I'm here," said the princess. "The wind picked me up and carried me here. I couldn't help it."

When the woman heard this, she said, "Come on up, I'll take care of you."

"How can I?" said Neea. "I can't climb the pole."

Then the old woman took a pair of shears and cut off some of her long, gray hair. She wove it into a rope and dropped one end down to the girl. She said, "Hold on, and I'll pull you up." Neea took hold of the rope, and the old woman pulled her up into the house. As soon as she got there, the princess told the old woman all about what the wind had done. The old woman listened to her and said, "You can stay here and help me. But when my daughters come, you'll have to hide. They may kill you if you don't." She made the princess take off her beautiful dress and burn it up. In its place she gave the girl a little blue dress. And the two of them set to work to bake some bread for supper.

After a time the old woman said, "My daughters will be here soon. You had better hide. Get in the wood box. There's a hole you can peek out of." So Neea got into the wood box, put down the lid, and looked out through the hole.

In a minute the house shook and turned. The old woman ran and opened the door, and in blew some one in a light blue cloak. Again the house did the same, only it turned in another direction, and another person came in. This happened four times in all. Then the old woman unbuttoned the cloaks for the four people who had come in; and there stood four girls, each of them one of the winds. They said to their mother, "Hurry up and give us supper. We are hungry and can't stay long." So the old woman put the supper on the table, and they sat down and ate.

One of the girls asked, "Did any one come here to-day?"

The old woman said, "Why do you ask that? You know no one ever comes here. How would they get here?"

The girl said, "I picked up a princess in a beautiful dress. I carried her here and left her not far from the house. Didn't she come?"

When the old woman heard these words that her daughter spoke, she went to the wood box and let Neea out. The girls were very glad to see the princess. They said, "We want you to live with us for a while. Do you want to live with us?"

Neea said, "I'd love to. Will you teach me to fly with you?"

The girls said, "We will. We'll take you everywhere we go."

So Neea stayed at the house of the four winds. The old woman made her a pale blue cloak just the same as the other girls had. And when the princess put it on, she was able to fly along with the winds wherever they went. And every day, for all day long, she went with them. She traveled from one end of the world to the other; she saw everything there was to see. She helped blow sail boats across the ocean. She helped rustle the leaves in the trees. She helped make rain-storms and snow-storms. All this she did. But always at night she flew back to the blue house on the pole and stayed with the old woman.

Neea was very happy. She came to love the four winds; and they made a sister of her. But they never let her fly alone, one of them always went with her. And they were very careful not to take her by the palace where her mother and father lived. All the time Neea grew stronger and stronger until she was just as strong as her brother and could do anything she wanted.

One day the winds had left her at home with the old woman. As she sat there, she was seized with a great longing to see her family. She wanted to fly by the palace and look at them, that was all. But none of the girls were there to take her. Even if one of them had been, she would not have done it. Neea thought to herself, "I can fly as well alone as I can with one of the winds. Why don't I put on my cloak and go?" She waited until the old woman was busy putting some bread in the oven. Then she jumped up, put on her cloak, and was out of the house in a hurry. The old woman called to her and told her to come back. But Neea paid no heed; she flew away from the blue land and went down to earth where the emperor and empress lived.

When she reached the palace, she saw her mother in the garden. So she swept down and flew by very close to her. Then she went and peeped in the window at her father, the emperor. While she was doing this, her brother felt the wind and ran out in the fields to fly his kite. Neea, seeing what he was doing, flew over and took hold of the kite. Higher and higher she pulled it, until the boy had no more string in his hands. Then she swept it this way and that way and made her brother run after it through the fields. The boy shouted and laughed, for he had never had such sport. But before Neea could see what was happening, she got all tangled up in the tail of the kite and could not get away. She struggled and pulled for all she was worth, but she could not break free. Then the boy began to pull the kite down. The harder he pulled, the harder Neea fought against him. So he called to his father and said, "Father, come help me. If you don't, my new kite will blow away." The emperor came running out of the palace and took hold of the string. The two of them pulled and pulled, and they did make the kite come down a little.

When the empress heard them shouting and saw them pulling, she came and said, "What's the matter? Can't you two pull down a kite?"

The emperor said, "Something has caught it up in the sky."

The empress said, "Don't be foolish. What could catch it in the sky? Here, let me help." And she took hold of the string and pulled.

With a great deal of pulling, the three of them at last got the kite near the ground. While the other two held on to the string, the empress reached up and caught hold of the tail. The minute she touched it, Neea's blue cloak disappeared; and she fell right on the ground in front of her mother. So surprised were the emperor and empress, that they could not believe their eyes. But Neea spoke to them and told them she was their daughter. Then she told them all about what had happened to her. They said, "Where is your beautiful dress?"

She said, "No one who does anything can wear a dress like that."

And the emperor and empress were glad to have their daughter back. She was so strong and so well that they let her run and play with the prince. And never after that did they make her wear such silly-looking clothes.

AT THE END of the story, the king said, "It's true that The Mouse knows of wonderful things. We have not heard such a story before. Surely it should open the Door."

But in spite of what the king said, the story did not

open the Door. The guards came forward and seized poor Punda-Poo and carried him off to the dungeon. He did not struggle; he did not protest; he did not say a word. He only thought, "This is what happens to me for talking. I'd have been much better off, if I'd never said a word."

CHAPTER XIX

NOOM-ZOR-NOOM AND THE STORY OF THE GREAT GIANT BUNGGAH

FOUR MEN had told their stories, and all four had failed. Noom-Zor-Noom was left alone waiting for the trumpet to sound. He lifted one corner of the golden cloth that covered the crystal block and whispered to Tal, "We are going before the king now. The other story-tellers have failed and have all been thrown into prison. If I don't open the Golden Door, you and I are lost. But, no matter what happens, you must keep absolutely quiet. The king must never know that I have brought you into Troom."

"He never will," said Tal. "I won't make a sound."

"Are you sure you're not too cramped?" asked Noom-Zor-Noom.

"I have lots of room," said Tal. "I like it here."

Then the trumpet sounded. Noom-Zor-Noom put his arm around Millitinkle's neck, and together they walked into the throne-room. When the courtiers saw the old man come in with his donkey, they burst out laughing, for they had never seen such a sight before. But the king was in no such humor: he was angry. He said, "Who are you, Noom-Zor-Noom, that you come before me with a donkey?"

"I could do nothing else, your highness," said the old man. "My stories are written on this crystal block. The block is too heavy for me to carry. So I brought it here on my donkey's back."

"Your stories!" said the king. "What do you mean by those words? I only asked for *one* story."

Then Noom-Zor-Noom told the king about the stories, how he had collected them and written them down on a crystal block. He said, "I am going to read you the best one of all that I have heard."

"Who ever said anything about reading a story?" said the king, beside himself with rage. "My orders were that you tell one."

"I know it," said Noom-Zor-Noom. "But . . ."

"But . . . nothing," said the king. "You have disobeyed my orders. You know what the penalty is for that."

"I could not have learned them all by heart," said Noom-Zor-Noom. "There are too many."

"That makes no difference," said the king. "My orders are my orders, and you should have obeyed them. You will only waste our time. It will do no good to read the story, not even if it's the best story in the world. The Golden Door wishes to have the story told."

King Tazzarin was so angry that he had about made up his mind to have the guards throw Noom-Zor-Noom into prison right away. At that point Millitinkle flapped her ears; the golden bells tinkled; and she said, "O king, please let my master read his story. It will open the Golden Door." Then she dropped a courtesy and stood looking at the king with her eyes wide open.

The king was so amused at the sight of a donkey that could talk and courtesy, that he forgot his anger. He said, "That is a wonderful donkey you have. How did she learn to talk?"

"I'll tell you," said Noom-Zor-Noom. And, while the king and courtiers listened, he told them about Millitinkle and the Snow Queen.

The king was so pleased with what the old man told, that he said, "If your stories are as good as that, you may read one. But that doesn't alter the fact that you have disobeyed my orders. Therefore, if you fail to open the Door, you must pay for your failure with your life. If you are willing to accept this condition, you may read your story."

Noom-Zor-Noom thought for a moment. Then he said, "I am willing to pay whatever penalty you exact. It makes no difference."

Millitinkle knelt down and the old man lifted the crystal block off her back and set it on the floor in front of the throne. He pulled back one corner of the golden cloth, just enough to uncover the story he wished to read: he left the rest covered up. Then he himself sat on the floor and read the story of

THE GREAT GIANT BUNGGAH

ONCE a mountain named Khar that lived at the bottom of the sea began to grow. It grew and grew, until it was so tall that it stuck its head right out of the water. After that it grew some more, so that to all the world it looked like nothing but a very high island. But it was different from most islands, because it was made of pink coral, and because it rose from the surface of an emerald sea. The sun always shone on Khar: the weather was always warm: and the many miles of beach that ran around the island were covered with smooth, pink sand.

Along the beaches, and for quite a distance up the slopes of Khar, grew thousands of Pentekka trees with slender trunks and big, silvery-blue leaves. From their branches hung the ripe Pentekkas—a sweet, juicy fruit the size and shape of a cocoanut and the color of a pearl. These Pentekkas were all that the people of Khar had to eat. Yet they wanted nothing more, for one Pentekka was enough to keep a man from being hungry for a year. So every spring, when the fruit ripened, each islander ate his Pentekka; and after that he ate no more until the fruit again became ripe. For this reason the islanders had no food to grow and no cooking to do. All day long they played on the pink beach, swam in the emerald sea, and stretched out under the warm sun that poured down on the marvelous island of Khar.

No one knows how long the people of Khar lived this

happy life. One day, however, a black speck appeared in the sky far out over the sea. As it came nearer, it grew in size, so that it soon looked like a big, black cloud. The islanders, who had never seen anything of the kind before, ran to the beach and stood gazing up into the sky. At first they were held in wonder, but this soon changed to fear; and all they could imagine was that a horrible monster was coming to eat them up. The more they looked, the more frightened they became, especially when they saw the black shadow of the monster skimming directly towards them across the calm waters of the sea. They watched as long as they dared; then all but the bravest ran and hid among the branches of the Pentekka trees.

Those few who stayed on the beach huddled together, waiting to see what would happen. Nearer and nearer the cloud came, until it was directly over the top of Khar. There it stopped and hovered a few feet above the highest point of the mountain. So thick and so black was the cloud, that it shut off all the sun and cast a deep shadow over the whole island. The next minute it lowered and touched the peak. When it lifted again, the people saw the huge figure of a giant sitting on the mountain top. Then a voice like thunder roared and said, "Happy people of Khar, you shall share your happiness with me. Behold, I am the great two-faced giant whom people call Bunggah. Here I shall stay and eat your Pentekkas, until a man of Khar is brave and strong enough to beat me in battle." And as he spoke, thunder clapped, lightning flashed, and rain poured down on the island.

When the rain began to come down, even the brave men who had stood on the beach ran to shelter under the Pentekka trees. And a great fear seized the hearts of all the people of Khar. "What can this mean?" they asked one another. "What have we done to deserve such punishment?" They peeped out from under the leaves of the trees hoping to see that the cloud had gone. But all that day and the next the rain poured down without stopping. And not once did the sun shine on the island of Khar.

On the third day Bunggah shouted, "If fifty men, each carrying a Pentekka, will come to me, I'll stop the rain."

At first the people did not know what to do. Then they decided to take the fruit to Bunggah. So fifty men each picked a Pentekka; they balanced them on their heads; and slowly they made their way up the mountain side to where the giant sat. Just as they reached the top of Khar, the rain stopped.

Bunggah greeted them kindly, saying, "I have not come to harm you. I have only come to share your happiness. Do not be afraid." But how could the people help being afraid? For Bunggah was a sight to see. He was a huge giant, and his body was all covered with blue hair. He wore a yellow tunic studded with sharks' teeth, and in his hand he held a club. Intead of one face, he had two, so that he could look both ways, behind and in front. His eyes were fiery red, and his mouth was big enough to hold a whole Pentekka at once. When the islanders saw him, they stood trembling with fear. Not one of them dared to say a word.

"Put the Pentekkas right here," said the giant, pointing to a spot on the ground in front of the bowlder on which he sat. The men did as he told them. They piled the Pentekkas on the ground and waited to see what the giant would do. "Fine," he said. "Just what I want for breakfast." One by one he put the Pentekkas in his mouth and swallowed them whole. And, without stopping to chew or speak, he ate up the whole pile of fruit in the wink of an eye. Then he smacked his lips and said, "I'll have fifty of these every day. And every day you bring them, it won't rain. But if you don't bring them, it will rain. And I shall keep my cloud over the island so as to have it ready in case I don't get my Pentekkas. Once a year, at the time of the ripening of the Pentekkas, I shall fight your bravest man. If he can beat me, I shall leave. If not, I shall stay for another year. That's all I have to say. You may go."

The people walked away and went down the mountain and joined their companions.

As soon as the rest of the islanders heard what the fifty had to say, they became sad. They did not know what to do. If there were no sun, the Pentekkas would not grow. If Bunggah ate fifty every day, there would not be any left for any one else. "We shall all starve," they said. "How can he mean that he has not come to do us harm?" And they went about their business sadly, for there was no more joy in their hearts.

The sun shone no more on Khar. The Pentekkas grew badly; only a few of them ripened; and these few were saved for Bunggah. The people lived on green fruit and were sick. No one played on the beaches, no one swam in the sea, no one laughed, and no one sang. Every day they took the fruit up the mountain; and once a year they sent their bravest man to fight Bunggah. Always he was beaten, for the giant was strong and his club was heavy, to say nothing of his being able to look in two directions at once. Though the man of Khar always fought bravely, he could do nothing. Bunggah just laughed at him and jeered at him and ended the fight by seizing the islander's club, snapping it in half, and sending the man home with these words: "If there is no one stronger than you, I shall stay forever. This is an easy life." Then there would follow another year without sun. For five years the people lived in this misery, until they did not care whether they lived or died.

About that time there were twins on the island of Khar. They were boys, and their names were Inggen-Nogg and Enggen-Nogg. They looked so much alike that no one could tell them apart, not even their own mother. They always lived together and played together, and they spoke a language of their own. When it came time for a man to be chosen to fight Bunggah at the end of the sixth year, Inggen-Nogg went to the people and said, "This year let me fight the giant. I am not strong, but I think I can beat him."

The people were surprised and said, "What makes you think you can beat the giant? He is strong, and you are weak. He will only laugh at you. We may as well send no one as you. You can do nothing without your brother."

"Perhaps not," said Inggen-Nogg. "But no one else has been able to do anything. Let me try. If I fail, you may cut my head off. If not, I shall ask for nothing."

When the people heard how earnest he was, they decided to let him fight the giant. But they had little faith in him. And some even went so far as to laugh at the boy, saying that he was young and foolish and thought too much of himself. But Inggen-Nogg paid no attention to them. He went off and joined Enggen-Nogg, and together they made ready for the fight.

Inggen-Nogg spent days hewing as heavy a club as he could swing. And, though the people did not know it, Enggen-Nogg hewed one too. After that the twins went off where no one could see them, and they practiced using the clubs until both became very skillful. Time passed, only one day was left before the fight. That night, while the rest of the islanders slept, the twins went secretly to that place where the men had piled the

U

Pentekkas that were to be carried to Bunggah in the morning. With great care they opened each Pentekka, cleaned it out, and filled it with pebbles. Then they put the fruit back together, so that not even the sharpest eye could see that a single Pentekka had been touched. This they did; and they went home to sleep.

In the morning Inggen-Nogg came to lead the men up the mountain. Enggen-Nogg was not to be seen; no one knew where he was. The men who carried the Pentekkas complained how heavy they were. "It's your own strength that's failing," said Inggen-Nogg; and the men really believed what he said. Up the mountain they went and piled their fruit in front of Bunggah. When the giant felt the Pentekkas, he was pleased and said, "Your fruit has ripened well." And he ate it all with an appetite.

The time came for the fight. Inggen-Nogg stepped forward, while the others stood by to see what would happen. Bunggah got up. But he was so full of pebbles that he moved slowly and with much trouble. The minute Inggen-Nogg advanced to attack him, Enggen-Nogg appeared from over the other side of the mountain. So much alike were the twins in every way that the two-faced giant thought he was only looking at one person. This confused him. How could the same person be in front of him and behind him at the same time? He rubbed his eyes and looked more carefully. And every time he looked, first Inggen-Nogg struck him, then Enggen-Nogg. Bunggah turned this way and that, but always, no matter what he did, one of the twins was attacking him from behind and the other from in front. This made him mad. He strutted about furiously, striking here and there with blows that meant to kill. But he was sluggish and heavy, and his aim was poor. The twins fought with all their might. They pounded the giant on the stomach, they pounded him on the back, and their clubs struck him with dull, sickening thuds. Bunggah shouted and taunted them about their weakness. He said, "You are a wonderful man to be on both sides of me at the same time. But what good will it do you? I can hardly feel your blows. Hit me harder." Then he stood still, raised his arms, and let Inggen-Nogg hit him for all he was worth. "Hit me again!" he shouted. "I didn't feel that at all." Inggen-Nogg hit him again, and again, and again. "Now," said the giant, hit me first on one side and then on the other." And he spread his legs, so that Inggen-Nogg could run between them. Then Inggen-Nogg and Enggen-Nogg hit him, one after the other, in such quick succession that their blows seemed to fall at the same time. Bunggah smiled and said, "You are doing well. Keep it up. It helps me digest the Pentekkas." But all of a sudden the pebbles began to pain him. A look of anguish came over his face and he said, "Enough! Stop it!" And

when the twins did not stop, Bunggah once more began
to fight. The harder he fought, the more the pebbles
pained him; and he really thought Inggen-Nogg was
hitting him hard enough to hurt. This frightened him,
for never before had such a thing happened. The pain
grew worse and worse, until at last the giant doubled up
and fell writhing on the ground. His club rolled out
of his hand, and he groaned in agony. The next minute
the twins picked up his club and pounded poor Bunggah
so hard on the stomach that he cried for mercy. "I'll
go, I'll go," he groaned. "Stop! I'll do anything you
want. I'll go!"

Inggen-Nogg said, "Call your cloud, and I'll let you
go."

Then Bunggah called for his cloud. The cloud lowered over the peak, and when it lifted, Bunggah was
gone. The cloud drifted away, and the sun shone again.
And once more the people of Khar enjoyed that happiness that had always been theirs. Inggen-Nogg and
Enggen-Nogg were made kings. And all the people of
Khar are alive and happy to-day.

FOR SOME little time after the story was finished, the
king and the queen, and the courtiers sat staring at
Noom-Zor-Noom. They could not take their eyes off
the man who had read such a wonderful story. Yet,
though all seemed intent on nothing but the story-teller,
at the same time they were listening for the Golden Door

THE NEXT MINUTE THE TWINS PICKED UP HIS CLUB AND POUNDED POOR
BUNGGAH SO HARD ON THE STOMACH THAT HE CRIED FOR MERCY.

to open. But they heard nothing, for the Door did not budge. At last the king looked at the Door. When he saw that it was still tight shut, he was disappointed and angry. He said to Noom-Zor-Noom, "Your story was a good one. If you had told it instead of read it, I think that the Door might have opened. You did not obey my orders, and now I must suffer for another year. But you will suffer too. You must pay the penalty: your head must come off."

When Noom-Zor-Noom heard what King Tazzarin said, he did not know what to do. He thought to himself, "This serves me right. I never should have brought Tal with me. How can I save him?" He looked at Millitinkle, as if she could help him out. But she was standing there dumbfounded, with her eyes on the floor; for the last thing she ever expected was that the Door would not open. Then the old man said to the king, "I have failed, and I am willing to die. But before I am beheaded, I should like to ask one thing of you."

"What is it?" asked the king.

"That you put the crystal block back on my donkey's back and let her go where she wishes," said Noom-Zor-Noom.

"I'll kill you both," said the king in his anger. "One of you is as bad as the other."

"I want to die with my master," said Millitinkle, quite forgetting about Tal.

"You may," said the king. Then he turned to the

guards and said, "Take this man out and behead him. Take his donkey with him too. I wish to see nothing more of either of them."

As soon as the king spoke, three guards rushed forward. Two of them started to carry Noom-Zor-Noom out of the room, and the other one led Millitinkle. They did not touch the crystal block; they left it lying on the floor in front of the throne. But before they reached the door, the king shouted in his rage, "Wait! Don't take him away until he has seen his crystal block smashed to bits before his own eyes."

Noom-Zor-Noom and Millitinkle tried to say something, but the guards would not let them speak. Then another guard was called, and he came forward with a sledge-hammer to smash the crystal block. While Noom-Zor-Noom and all the others looked on in breathless silence, the guard raised his hammer and brought it down with all his force on to the crystal block. There was a crash; all the candles went out; and the room became dark. And above the murmur of many voices, could be heard the king shouting, "What has happened? Why did the candles go out?"

He had just finished these words, when the Golden Door began to glow. As it glowed, one of the eyes in the golden head lit up so bright that it cast a beam of light across the room. Then slowly, little by little, the Door swung open. And as it opened, the beam of light from the eye swept across the room, until it shone on the spot where the crystal block had been smashed. There it stopped, casting its bright light on Tal, who sat among the broken bits of crystal. For a moment no one said a word, no one breathed. And before the king could realize what had really happened, the golden head spoke and said, "There is your son. He has come back to you."

Then the queen shouted, "It's our boy!" And she rushed down to where Tal was sitting. The king followed behind her, forgetting his dignity and stumbling along as best he could in all his robes. They took hold of Tal and kissed him and hugged him until he was almost smothered. And every one else in the room crowded around as close as they could get.

Meanwhile the eye stopped shining; the door shut; and the candles began to burn again. So intent was every one on the boy who came out of the crystal block, that no one even thought to look behind the Golden Door. When they did think of it, it was too late. And, though some of them tried to make it open again, it would not move.

After his first joy at seeing the boy was over, the king called to the guards and made them bring Noom-Zor-Noom before him. He looked at the old man and asked, "Did you bring this boy in?"

"I did," said Noom-Zor-Noom.

"Where did he come from?" asked the king.

"I brought him with me from a place called Martoona," said Noom-Zor-Noom. And he went on and told the king all he knew about Tal.

"You did well," said the king. "You and your donkey are free."

After that there was a great deal of talking and a great deal of confusion. And soon the word spread throughout Troom that the king's son had come back.

So Tal turned out to be King Tazzarin's son. He became the prince that he really was. All the story-tellers were freed from prison. Noom-Zor-Noom was made vizier; and he and Millitinkle were given one of the best rooms in the palace. King Tazzarin, now that he had his son back, became the good and kind man that he had been before the prince disappeared. He ruled his people well and made them happy.

The first night that Tal was home with his mother and father, he told them all about Martoona. And when the king and queen heard how well he had been treated in that village, they sent to Martoona and brought all the people to Troom. King Tazzarin gave them houses and money and everything else to make them happy. And they lived as well as they deserved to live.

Tal, Noom-Zor-Noom, and Millitinkle never forgot their trip to Troom. They still talk about it and laugh about the time Tal became part giraffe. Millitinkle has become a little less argumentative—but not much.

AND BEFORE THE KING COULD REALIZE WHAT HAD REALLY HAPPENED, THE
GOLDEN HEAD SPOKE AND SAID, "THERE IS YOUR SON."

To-day Tal is king; and his title is King Tazzarin, the Second, the Greatest King of Troom. So far the Golden Door has never opened again, not even for Tal. And to this day no one knows what is behind it.

PAUL FENIMORE COOPER, a great-grandson of the novelist James Fenimore Cooper, was born in Albany, New York, in 1899 and graduated from Yale in 1921. His other books included *Tricks of Women and Other Albanian Tales* (1928), a translation of folk tales; *Island of the Lost* (1961), a non-fiction account of the Arctic expedition of Sir John Franklin, and *Dindle* (1964), another book for children, about a dwarf who saves a kingdom from a dragon.

He lived in Cooperstown, New York, with his wife Marion Erskine Cooper and their son Paul, Jr., a physicist and Arctic explorer. The author died in 1970.